Red Sky in  ....

Born in Gainsborough, Lincolnshire, Margaret Dickinson moved to the coast at the age of seven and so began her love for the sea and the Lincolnshire landscape. Her ambition to be a writer began early and she had her first novel published at the age of twenty-five. This was followed by a number of further titles including *Plough the Furrow*, *Sow the Seed* and *Reap the Harvest*, which make up her Lincolnshire Fleethaven trilogy.

Many of her novels are set in the heart of her home county but in *Tangled Threads* and *Twisted Strands*, the stories include not only Lincolnshire but also the framework knitting and lace industries of Nottingham.

Her 2012 and 2013 novels, *Jenny's War* and *The Clippie Girls*, were both top-twenty bestsellers and her 2014 and 2015 novels, *Fairfield Hall* and *Welcome Home*, were both *Sunday Times* top-ten bestsellers.

ALSO BY MARGARET DICKINSON

Plough the Furrow

Sow the Seed

Reap the Harvest

The Miller's Daughter

Chaff upon the Wind

The Fisher Lass

The Tulip Girl

The River Folk

Tangled Threads

Twisted Strands

Without Sin

Pauper's Gold

Wish Me Luck

Sing As We Go

Suffragette Girl

Sons and Daughters

Forgive and Forget

Jenny's War

The Clippie Girls

Fairfield Hall

Welcome Home

Margaret Dickinson

Red Sky in the Morning

PAN BOOKS

First published 2004 by Pan Books

This edition published 2016 by Pan Books
an imprint of Pan Macmillan
20 New Wharf Road, London N1 9RR
Associated companies throughout the world
www.panmacmillan.com

ISBN 978-1-5098-0909-7

Copyright © Margaret Dickinson, 2004

The right of Margaret Dickinson to be identified as the
author of this work has been asserted by her in accordance
with the Copyright, Designs and Patents Act 1988.

All rights reserved. No part of this publication may be reproduced,
stored in a retrieval system, or transmitted, in any form, or by any means
(electronic, mechanical, photocopying, recording or otherwise)
without the prior written permission of the publisher.

Pan Macmillan does not have any control over, or any responsibility for,
any author or third party websites referred to in or on this book.

1 3 5 7 9 8 6 4 2

A CIP catalogue record for this book is available from the British Library.

Typeset by SetSystems Ltd, Saffron Walden, Essex
Printed and bound by CPI Group (UK) Ltd, Croydon, CR0 4YY

This book is sold subject to the condition that it shall not, by way of
trade or otherwise, be lent, hired out, or otherwise circulated without
the publisher's prior consent in any form of binding or cover other than
that in which it is published and without a similar condition including
this condition being imposed on the subsequent purchaser.

Visit www.panmacmillan.com to read more about all our books
and to buy them. You will also find features, author interviews and
news of any author events, and you can sign up for e-newsletters
so that you're always first to hear about our new releases.

For Zoë and Scott,

my daughter and son-in-law

Acknowledgements

My grateful thanks to Graham and Liz Jarnell for answering all my questions about sheep. Any errors, of course, are mine and not theirs! As always, my love and thanks go to my family and friends, especially my husband, Dennis, and those who read the script in the early stages: Robena and Fred Hill, David and Una Dickinson, Linda and Terry Allaway and Pauline Griggs. Your constant support and encouragement mean more to me than you can ever know.

Special thanks to the best agent any writer could have – Darley Anderson. Thank you, too, to all the 'team' at Macmillan, headed by my lovely editor, Imogen Taylor. You're all absolutely wonderful.

1946

One

The girl was standing in the middle of the cobbled marketplace. She had been there for hours whilst the busy market bustled around her. All day the raucous shouts of the stallholders had rung out, each vying with the others to attract the attention of the shoppers, but they had not gained hers. It was two weeks before Christmas and the stalls were laden with holly wreaths and mistletoe, bringing colour to a drab, wet day.

Now it was growing dark and the traders were packing up and going home. Home to a warm fire and a hot drink, no doubt liberally laced with whisky to drive out the chill and to thaw frozen hands and feet. The rain had been falling steadily since early morning and the girl, just standing there so quiet and still, staring ahead of her and looking neither to right nor left, was soaked to her skin. Her long black hair was plastered against her head. The bottom button of the shapeless coat she wore was missing and the garment flapped open, revealing the swelling mound of her belly. Yet she didn't seem to care about her condition, or even about the discomfort she must be feeling. She seemed unaware of everything and everyone around her. Her thin face was white and pinched with cold, and devoid of expression. Her blue eyes, so dark they were almost violet, were lifeless.

'A' ya goin' to stand there all night, lass?' The last

market trader to load his wares into the back of an old van shouted across the wet cobblestones, shining now in the pale glow from the street lamp. She did not even glance in his direction. It was as if she hadn't heard him. The man wiped the back of his hand across his face and shrugged. 'Please ya'sen,' he muttered and turned away. He looked longingly towards the public house, the Shepherd's Crook. Even out here in the cold and the wet, the buzz of conversation could be heard through the open door. A haze of pipe and cigarette smoke drifted out into the night air. The market trader hesitated for a moment, seemingly torn between the inviting hospitality the place offered and the thought of home, where his wife would be waiting with a hot meal and warm slippers. The pull of home won and he bent to swing the starting handle of his battered van. The engine spluttered into life and he moved to the driver's side of the vehicle, slinging the starting handle into the well in front of the passenger seat. He glanced across at the girl, then shrugged again and climbed into the van.

When the noise of the motor had died away the marketplace was deserted, except for the girl. The only other living creature was a pony, harnessed to an old-fashioned trap and tethered outside the Shepherd's Crook. It looked as wet and miserable as the girl felt. Just once she licked her lips, tasting the rain.

The laughter and the noise from the pub spilled into the street as three men came out, lurching along the pavement, bumping into one another, laughing and joking and filled with the merriment of the festive season. They didn't even notice her. More men left the pub in twos and threes, yet the pony still stood there, occasionally pawing the ground, his metal-clad hoof scraping the cobbles. He shook his head and water droplets showered from his rain-soaked mane.

'Time to go home, Eddie. You can't stay here all night.' There was a disturbance in the doorway of the pub and, for the first time, the girl's glance focused on the two men there. One was very unsteady, reeling from side to side and being steered towards the waiting pony and trap by the other. 'Come on. Your pony'll tek you home. Good job he knows the way better'n you when you're in this state, in't it?'

For a moment the drunken man leant against the trap, then he grasped the side and, with the aid of the other man, heaved himself into the back. The pony lifted his head, perking up at once now his warm stable was almost in sight.

'On you go, then.' The publican raised his hand, about to untether the pony and slap its rump to send it on its way, when the man in the back mumbled, 'Wait. Wait a mo'.'

Through the blur of drink and the steadily falling rain, he had caught a glimpse of the girl standing in the middle of the square. He raised a shaking finger and pointed. 'Who's that?'

'Eh?' The landlord glanced over his shoulder. 'Oh, her. Bin there hours. Some tramp beggin', I 'spect. Well, she needn't think she's goin' to get a bed at my place.'

Eddie was scrambling out of the trap again.

'Now, now,' the other man remonstrated. 'On you go home, Eddie. You're goin' to be in enough trouble with your missis as it is. Don't be bothering yourself with the likes of that little trollop.'

Eddie shook off the man's restraining hand. 'You can't leave a poor lass standing there in this weather,' he mumbled and began to shamble towards the girl.

5

The landlord shrugged. 'Have it your way, then. I've better things to do with me time. Goodnight to you, Eddie Appleyard.'

The landlord went inside and slammed the heavy door of the public house. The sound of the bolts being shot home echoed in the silence.

Still the girl had not moved as Eddie reached her and stood before her, swaying slightly. He peered at her through the gloom. 'Nowhere to go, lass?' His voice was gentle and caring and the girl, who had thought she was empty of all emotion, felt tears prickle behind her eyelids. It was the first kind word she had heard in weeks, months even. Slowly, she shook her head.

He touched her arm lightly. 'Then you'd best come home with me.' Without waiting for any sign of agreement or otherwise from her, Eddie turned and reeled back towards the trap. But before he reached it, he stumbled and fell to the cobbles. The girl watched for a moment and then, when he made no attempt to rise, she moved at last. Her limbs were stiff with cold and for the first few steps she hobbled like an old woman. She bent and grasped his arm. He grunted and, leaning heavily on her, struggled to his feet. They staggered towards the trap. The man scrambled into the back and then turned, holding out his hand towards her. 'Come on, lass. You can't stay out here all night.'

She hesitated and then put her hand into his. When she was sitting beside him on the floor he said, 'Giddup, Duke.' The pony moved and, as the trap swayed, the girl clung on to the side, but the man merely shifted himself into a more comfortable position. Curling his body to fit into the confined space, he lay down. With a satisfied grunt, he rested his head on her lap and, almost at once, began to snore.

The pony bent its head against the driving rain as it plodded up the steep hill, leaving the lights of the town behind them. Beneath the slight shelter the sides of the trap afforded and with the warmth of the man close to her seeping into her chilled being, the girl's eyelids closed. Her head drooped forward and soon, draped across the man, she too slept.

Two

'Who the hell's this?'

A woman's strident voice startled the girl awake. The pony and trap had come to a halt in the middle of a farmyard. Farm buildings and a house loomed through the darkness. The woman, a raincoat over her head, was standing at the back of the trap, poking the sleeping man with her forefinger.

'Eddie – wake up. Who's this, I'd like to know? Some trollop you've picked up at the market?' She prodded him viciously. 'You've a nerve and no mistake. Come on.' She began to pull at him. 'Stir ya'sen. I want an explanation. And it'd better be good.'

The man grunted and lifted his head. His face now on a level with the woman's, he murmured, 'Bertha, my dearly beloved wife.' He grinned foolishly, but even in his drunken state the girl could detect the sarcasm in his tone.

'I'll "beloved wife" you,' the woman shrilled as she dragged him from the trap. He fell to the ground on his hands and knees, but she made no effort to help him up. Instead she pushed him with her toe. 'Get up, ya daft beggar. And as for you,' she added, glaring up at the girl still sitting on the floor of the trap, 'you can be on ya way—'

'No – no.' Hanging on to the back of the trap, the man dragged himself upright. He swayed slightly, but his voice was less slurred now. 'No, she's stayin'. She's nowhere to go.'

'What's that to do with you? Who is she?'

The man shrugged. 'Dunno. She was standing in the marketplace getting soaking wet, so I brought her home.'

'Oh, a real knight in shining armour, aren't ya? Get on inside.' The woman pushed him again. Then she jabbed her finger towards the girl. 'And you. You'd better come inside an' all. Only for a minute, mind. I want to get to the bottom of this.'

The woman, small and very overweight, nevertheless marched towards the back door of the farmhouse with surprising agility.

'Come on, lass,' Eddie said. 'We'd better do as she says.' He held out his hand to her and, stiffly, she climbed out of the trap. As they began to walk towards the house, the girl spoke for the first time. Her voice was low and husky.

'What about the pony?'

'Eh?' Eddie blinked. 'Oh aye.' He lurched back towards the animal, still waiting patiently, and patted its neck. 'Poor old Duke. You always get the rough end of the stick, don't you?' His voice was low as he muttered, 'Reckon we both do.'

The man began to grapple with the harness and the girl moved to help him. As soon as the pony felt himself released from the shafts, he trotted towards the building on the right-hand side of the yard. The man gave a wry laugh. 'He knows his way home all right.'

They left the trap in the middle of the yard and went towards the house.

'If she – if she won't let you stay in the house, lass, the hayloft above Duke's stable is dry and in the morning—' He wiped his hand across his face and then shook his head as if trying to clear it. 'I'm not thinking too straight, but I'll sort summat out for you in the morning.' They stepped into a scullery and through that into a warm kitchen, where the smell of freshly baked mince pies still lingered. 'I'll see if I can get her to—'

'So? What's all this about?' Bertha was standing with her fat arms folded across her bosom. Her mousy coloured hair was straight and roughly cut into an untidy bob. Parted on one side, the long section of hair was held back from her face by a grip. Her florid cheeks were lined with tiny red veins and her mouth was small, the thin lips lost in the fatness of her face. Only in her mid-thirties, yet already she had a double chin. As she stood awaiting her husband's explanation, her pale hazel eyes sparked with anger.

Behind the woman, in the doorway leading further into the house, stood a young boy in striped flannelette pyjamas. He was no more than ten years old and his large brown eyes were darting from one to the other between his parents, but they seemed oblivious to his presence.

The girl shivered and glanced towards the glowing fire, longing to kneel before it and hold out her hands to its heat.

'Well? I'm waiting.' The woman's glance raked the girl, taking in her bedraggled state. Then her mouth turned down in disgust. 'I might 'ave known. She's in the family way. Is it yours, Eddie Appleyard?'

'Don't talk daft, woman.' Her accusation brought a brief spark of retaliation. 'I ain't even seen her afore tonight.'

'Huh! Expect me to believe that.' She stepped towards

the girl. 'Well, you can be on your way, whoever you are.'

The man said nothing, but he made a motion with his head as if to remind the girl of his earlier offer for her to sleep in the hayloft.

'I saw that. Ee, there's more going on here than you're letting on. I can tell.'

Eddie ran his hand agitatedly through his thick brown hair. He was a tall, thin man in his mid-thirties, yet slightly stooping, as if the years of farm work were already bending his back. His face was weather-beaten and there were lines around his brown eyes.

'There's nothing going on, as you put it,' he said wearily. 'She's just a poor lass who's got nowhere to go. Surely, you can show a bit of—'

'And why's she got nowhere to go?' Bertha flung her arm out, pointing at the girl's stomach. 'Because 'er family – if she's got any – has slung the little slut out, that's why.'

Eddie sighed. 'You don't know that.' They were talking about the girl as if she was not there. 'You don't know anything about her. No more than I do.'

'Aye, but I can guess.'

'It's the truth I'm telling you,' he said quietly, yet there was a note in his tone that implied he knew she wouldn't believe him.

Bertha turned towards the girl. 'What's your name then?'

The violet eyes regarded the woman steadily. 'Anna,' the girl said softly.

'Anna what?'

The girl hesitated and looked away, avoiding Bertha's probing, hostile eyes. She ran her tongue nervously round her lips. 'Anna Woods.'

But Bertha had noticed the hesitation. She sniffed in disbelief. 'Oh aye. Well then, Anna Woods – or whatever your name is – you'd better take yourself off, 'cos we don't want the likes of you hanging around here. Go on.' She flapped her hand. 'Be off with you. And don't come round here again.'

'She can sleep in the stable,' Eddie put in. 'You can't turn the lass out, specially when it's nearly Christmas.' Sadly, he added, 'No room at the inn, eh, Bertha? Now look, love, why don't you find her a blanket and—?'

'I aren't finding the little trollop owt.' Bertha whipped round on him. 'And as for you, Eddie Appleyard, you ain't heard the last of this.' At that moment she noticed the boy still standing in the doorway. Instantly Bertha's whole demeanour changed. She stepped towards him and put her arm around his shoulders. 'What are you doing down here, Tony? Go back to bed, there's a good boy.'

Anna saw the boy glance briefly at his father as he murmured, 'Yes, Mam,' and then he scuttled out of sight. She heard his light footsteps on the stairs and then the sound of his bare feet pattering across the floor above.

'There.' The woman rounded on her husband again. 'See how you upset him? He can't sleep till he knows you're safely home. He's the same every week. Though why he should bother himself after the way you carry on beats me.'

Sickened by the woman's ranting, Anna turned and stepped out of the warm kitchen and through the scullery. As she opened the back door, she shivered again as the coldness of the wet night hit her once more. She bent her head against the rain and hurried towards the barn door through which the pony had disappeared.

Halfway across the yard, she jumped as a dog, chained outside its kennel, barked and tried to run towards her. She couldn't see it clearly in the darkness, but she made soothing sounds in her throat. The dog ceased its barking, whined and then returned to its shelter. *Even he doesn't like the wet*, she thought wryly.

Inside the barn, it was cold but dry. As her eyes became accustomed to the dark, Anna felt her way around, her icy fingers touching the brick walls. She heard the sound of the pony and her fingers touched a coarse blanket thrown over the boarding at the side of his stall.

'Sorry, Duke,' she murmured and stroked his rump, 'but my need is greater than yours tonight.'

Hugging the blanket, which smelled strongly of horse, she felt her way up a ladder and into the hayloft. She removed her wet coat and wrapped herself in the blanket, then lay down on the hay, burrowing beneath it to find what warmth she could.

Exhausted, she was asleep in seconds.

Anna was awakened by the sound of someone climbing the ladder to the loft. She stretched and raised herself on one elbow. It was not the man whose head appeared, but the young boy's. They stared at each other for several moments in the pale light of a cold dawn, before Anna lay down again and closed her eyes. She hoped he would go away once his curiosity had been satisfied. She had not yet made up her mind what to do next. She wished she could stay here for ever. She was warm and snug for the first time in weeks.

In fact, she thought, *this would be a nice place to die.*

She was about to drift off into sleep again when she heard the boy climb the rest of the ladder and creep, on hands and knees, across the hay towards her. There was a long silence before he whispered, 'I've brought you something to eat.' Another pause and then he added, 'And some milk.'

She opened her eyes again and looked up at him. He was holding a roughly wrapped parcel and had a small milk can hooked over his wrist. 'It's only bread and cheese.' He was apologetic. 'It's all I could take without me mam finding out.'

Now Anna sat up, reaching out thankfully to take the food. She had been ready to give up, to succumb at last to an overwhelming desire to close her eyes and never wake up, but the physical ache of hunger revived her instinct to survive.

The boy watched her as she ate ravenously, his brown eyes large in his thin face. 'Are you going to have a baby?' The question was innocent enough, but the girl scowled at him and did not answer. Yet it was the first time her face had registered any kind of emotion. 'Where have you come from?' Again, no answer. 'Where are you going?' To this she replied only with a vague lift of her shoulders. 'Haven't you got a home? A mam and dad?'

Anna lay down again. 'Thanks for the food,' she said flatly, deliberately ignoring his questions. Her words were a dismissal, yet the boy did not move. He sat quietly beside her and she could feel him watching her.

They heard a noise below and, startled, the boy scrambled away towards the ladder. Anna raised her head. He was peering down the open hatch, his eyes wide and fearful. Then she saw him relax, the sudden tension in his limbs drain away.

'Hello, lad.' Eddie Appleyard's voice drifted up. 'Come to see if our visitor's still here, have you?'

The boy nodded as the man began to climb up towards him. 'I brought her some bread an' cheese, Dad. And some milk. But don't tell Mam, will you?'

Eddie appeared at the top of the ladder. Even through the poor light, Anna could see that he was smiling. He reached out and ruffled his son's hair. 'No, son, course I won't.' His grin broadened and Anna had the feeling it was not the first secret that father and son had shared. 'As long as you don't tell her I've raided the larder an' all.' He handed up a blue-and-white-check cloth bundle as he glanced across to where the girl lay. The boy took it and moved back to her side. 'Me dad's brought you something too.'

The man levered himself up the last rungs of the ladder and stepped into the loft, bending his head to avoid the low rafters. He dropped to his haunches beside her as, now, Anna sat upright.

'It's very kind of you,' she said huskily as she unwrapped the cloth. There was a slice of pork pie, two cold sausages and two slices of bread, spread thickly with butter.

'And here's a couple of apples,' the man said, fishing in his pocket. 'From our own orchard. We lay 'em out on newspaper in the loft to last us through the winter.'

Now they both sat and watched her eat. When she had finished, the man said kindly, 'Now, lass, what can we do to help you? Are you heading for somewhere? I could mebbe take you there, if it's not too far away?'

There was a long silence whilst the girl seemed to be struggling inwardly. She saw the man and his young son exchange a glance, but they waited patiently for her

15

answer. At last she said haltingly, 'No, I'm not going anywhere.'

'Are you looking for work?' Eddie asked. 'Is that it?'

'I suppose so, though—' She hesitated, before adding bitterly, 'I won't be able to work for very long.'

'Do you know owt about farm work?' Eddie asked, carefully ignoring her brief reference to her condition.

The girl regarded him steadily, seeming to weigh up the consequences of her answer before uttering it. Guardedly, she said, 'A bit.'

'Can you milk cows?'

She shook her head, her eyes downcast. Her reluctance was obvious, but at last she admitted, 'Sheep. I know about sheep.'

The boy clapped his hands excitedly. 'We've got sheep. Lincolnshire Longwools,' he added with a note of pride. 'And it'll be lambing time soon. She could help with the sheep, Dad, couldn't she?'

'Well—' Now the man was doubtful. 'I wasn't thinking so much of her staying with us.' His expression was both apprehensive and apologetic at the same time. 'I was just wondering if we could find her a place on a farm hereabouts.'

The boy's face fell.

'It's all right, Mister.' Anna moved to get up from her warm nest in the hay. 'I don't want to cause you any bother.' She glanced at him shrewdly as, remembering the previous night, she added softly, 'No more than I have already.' In a shaft of early morning light slanting through the rafters, she could see that Eddie had a scratch on his left cheekbone. A scratch that had not been there the previous evening.

Eddie made a dismissive gesture with his hand, but she could see the wariness deep in his eyes. The boy was still glancing from one to the other, biting his lip. Suddenly, his expression brightened again. 'What about the cottage, Dad? Couldn't she stay there?'

The man looked at him, at the girl and then back to his son. 'But it's nearly falling down, lad. It's hardly weatherproof.'

'You could mend it, Dad.' The boy's face was alight with eagerness. 'You could do the walls.' He glanced at Anna. 'They're only mud.' Now he looked back again to his father. 'And Mr Wainwright could do the roof.' Once more he explained to Anna, 'It's a thatched roof and Mr Wainwright does thatching. He mended the corner shop in the village. It's got a thatched roof an' all. Oh Dad, do let her stay. Please. She's got nowhere else to go.'

'Is that right, lass?' the man asked her quietly and when she nodded, he sighed.

His brow furrowed, he sat deep in thought for several minutes until a shout made them all jump. It was Bertha's shrill voice in the barn below them.

'Eddie? Where are you?'

The boy made a sudden movement like a startled fawn, but his father put his finger to his lips.

Bertha was at the bottom of the ladder. 'Are you up there, Eddie Appleyard? 'Cos if you are—'

It sounded as if the woman suspected that Anna had spent the night in the hayloft. Like statues the three of them were motionless, the boy holding his breath, his father looking guilty. Anna watched the man with detached curiosity. *He's afraid of her*, she thought with a flicker of surprise. Never before had she seen a man fearful of a woman. The other way about, yes, oh yes . . .

She closed her mind against thoughts that threatened to overwhelm her.

Bertha's voice, still calling her husband's name, was further away now. 'She'll be gone in a minute,' the man said in a low voice, 'then you can go down, Tony.'

'What if she asks where I've been?'

Eddie's smile flickered briefly. 'Well, I wouldn't tell her you've been up here with this lass. Don't worry, I don't think she'll ask you. It's me she's after.' He looked at Anna. 'She'll be wanting the trap harnessed. She always goes into the town on a Thursday to see her sister and do a bit of shopping.' He chuckled, a deep rumbling sound, and his face looked suddenly much younger, laughter lines wrinkling around his eyes. 'For all the things I've forgotten to bring from the market the day before when I've had one too many.'

He stood up and brushed the hay from his clothes. 'Come on, Tony. Time you were getting ready for school.' He turned back to Anna and smiled down at her. 'You stay here. When the wife's gone, I'll come back and take you down to the cottage.' He pulled a wry expression. 'But it's not much to look at.'

The man descended the ladder first and the boy followed, pausing briefly to smile back at her. Anna raised her hand and curled her fingers in a kind of wave, but could not summon an answering smile.

Three

'It's not much of a place,' Eddie said again as they walked up the slope away from the farm, 'but it's in a good spot near the woods. Sheltered, but very isolated.' Anna felt his glance. 'It'll be lonely for you.'

That'll suit me, she thought, though she said nothing.

She had waited in the hayloft until she heard the trap rattle out of the yard, the sound of its wheels on the roadway receding into the distance. Only a moment later she had heard the man calling softly from below. 'Coast's clear, lass.'

They walked on, but near the top of the hill Anna paused and looked back towards the farm where the man and his family lived. Cackle Hill Farm, for she had seen the name on the gate as they left, was set against a background of trees, beyond which was the rolling countryside of the Lincolnshire Wolds. She turned and followed the man, who was still plodding to the top of the rise. When they reached it, they both paused to take in the view below them. The land sloped away again and at the bottom of the track on this side of the hill Anna could see the outline of a cottage nestling against a wooded area on the right from where she was standing. The land was cold and stark, the trees naked against the grey sky, but in spring and summer she guessed the view would be idyllic. Just beyond the cottage she could see a stream bubbling down the hillside

19

and disappearing round the far side of the wood. Sheep dotted the sloping fields and, for the first time in weeks, Anna smiled.

'You like it?' Eddie asked gently. Anna jumped. For a moment she had forgotten he was there.

'Oh! Oh yes.' She nodded. 'It was the sheep. I – I like sheep,' she added diffidently.

Eddie nodded. 'Mek you feel at home, d'they?'

Her smile faded and at once her face took on a closed look. 'Something like that,' she murmured and the man knew he had said the wrong thing. Silently, he vowed not to mention her home, nor question her about her background. But he liked this lass. He wanted to help her. She was like a lost sheep herself and his tender heart reached out to her. He sighed. If only his wife would be as kindly disposed towards her.

They were nearing the cottage now and Anna could see that it was as tumbledown as he had said. It was a small, lime-washed, mud-and-stud, thatched building with a central front door and a window on either side. To the left of the door, there was a gaping hole where the mud had crumbled away, leaving the wooden slats of the framework exposed. On the same side of the cottage the thatched roof was badly in need of repair. Several of the windowpanes were broken and the front door leant drunkenly on its hinges. When Eddie pushed it open, it scraped the mud floor.

'This place is only used at lambing time. I stay here, specially if the weather's bad. My lad comes too – if his mam'll let him.' The last few words were murmured, almost as if he did not intend the girl to hear them.

The door opened into a tiny hallway with steep stairs, more like a ladder than a proper staircase, leading to the upper floor.

'It's two up and two down, but I only ever use this room,' Eddie said, leading her into the room to the right. He laughed as he jerked his thumb over his shoulder towards the other room. 'I put the sheep in yon one.' He stood looking about him. 'But it's not too bad in here. At least it's weatherproof. We'll get a fire going in there.' He nodded towards the grate, beside which, built into the brickwork, was a bread oven.

Anna glanced around. It was like stepping back into the last century – or maybe even the one before that. There were no rugs to clothe the coldness of the beaten-earth floor. In one corner there was a rusty iron bedstead, but there was no mattress on it. A wooden rocking chair stood near the fireplace, and in the centre of the room there was a table and one kitchen chair. But to the girl, who had lived rough for months in barns and outhouses, the promise of somewhere dry and warm was heaven-sent.

'It's a bit sparse.' Eddie smiled apologetically. 'But we don't need much when we stay here. Anyway, I'll fetch you the feather mattress I use. It's in our loft at the moment.' He pointed. 'That door there's the pantry. I'll soon get that stocked up for you. And this one' – he opened another door that led directly out of the kitchen at the side of the cottage – 'goes outside to the privy. It's down the path there. And you'll have to fetch your water from the stream, I'm afraid. But it's fresh and clean. Comes from a spring up the hill.'

Anna nodded.

'Like Tony said,' Eddie went on, 'I can repair the walls and the windows. I'll rehang the front door and I'll ask Joe Wainwright if he—'

'I can't pay for work to be done,' Anna said at once. Then, realizing she might have sounded ungrateful, she gestured with her hand and added, 'It's – it's very kind of you, but I – I have nothing.'

Gently, Eddie said, 'I wouldn't expect you to pay, lass. The cottage belongs to me and it's high time I got it repaired up.'

'But I can't afford to pay you rent, at least not at the moment.'

The man dismissed the idea. 'Don't you worry about that, love. Besides, you're going to help me with the lambing.' He paused significantly, as if he realized he was forcing her to make up her mind, before adding quietly, 'Aren't you?'

They regarded each other steadily for several moments before she nodded slowly.

When Tony arrived home from school it was already dusk. He rushed into the kitchen and skidded to a halt, surprised to see his mother standing behind the table unpacking her shopping. Before he could bite back the words, he said, 'You're home early. I didn't think you'd be back from Auntie Lucy's yet.'

Bertha smiled. 'I couldn't wait to get back to show you what I've bought you. Here – ' she held out a brown paper bag towards him – 'open it.'

Tony sat at the table. 'But it's not Christmas yet.'

His mother smiled at him. 'Oh, that's just a little extra one from your mam.'

Inside the bag was the usual bar of chocolate she always brought him after her trip to town, but today there was another present. A Dinky toy.

'Aw, Mam – thanks! It's that tractor I wanted.' He opened the box and ran the toy along the table, imitating the sound of a real vehicle. 'Chugger-chugger-chugger.'

Bertha watched him fondly. 'That's all right, love.' She sat down opposite him and rested her arms on the table. 'Now, tell me,' she said, 'what you've been doing at school today.'

'We had writing this morning and sums and then we played footie this after.' The boy reeled off the events of his day.

With deceptive mildness, Bertha asked, 'And did you enjoy the piece of pork pie and the cold sausages as well as the sandwiches I packed for you?'

The boy sat very still. His eyes were still on his new toy, but now he was not moving the tractor or imitating its sounds.

'You can tell your mam, Tony love. I won't be cross. I just want you to tell me if you took them. That's all.'

The boy's lower lip trembled. He opened his mouth once, then twice, but no sound came out. The back door opened and closed and there was the sound of Eddie removing his boots in the scullery.

He appeared in the doorway into the kitchen and stood there for a few moments, glancing between the two seated on either side of the table. 'What's up?'

'Nothing.' Bertha snapped. 'Me an' Tony are just having a little chat. That's all.'

'Oh aye. What've you been up to now, lad? Not in trouble at school, are you?' Eddie moved into the room and went to stand beside his son's chair. He smiled down at the boy and ruffled his hair. Tony shook his head but still did not speak. Instead he stared miserably at his new toy as if all the joy had been taken out of the gift. Eddie looked across the table at his wife, a question in his eyes.

'I was just asking him if he'd enjoyed the pork pie and sausages that's gone missing out of my meat safe in

23

the larder. That's all. Simple enough question, I'd've thought, but it seems as if he doesn't want to answer me.'

'Ah.' Eddie let out a long sigh. 'Now I get it.' Heavily, he said, 'Go out and feed the hens, there's a good boy. Me and ya mam need to talk.'

Tony scrambled from his chair, leaving his new toy on the table. Quietly he closed the door from the kitchen into the scullery, but he did not leave the house. Instead, he stood with his ear pressed to the closed door. He could hear every word clearly.

'You know very well the lad didn't take the food, but it's your way of trying to find out. You shouldn't *use* him, Bertha. It isn't his fault you an' me don't get on nowadays.'

'And whose fault is it, I'd like to know? *I* don't disappear off to market every week and come home rolling drunk, after being with goodness knows how many trollops in the town. And then you have the gall to bring one of 'em home with you. Into my house.' She beat her chest with her fist.

Wearily, Eddie said, 'Bertha, I don't go with trollops, as you put it. In fact, I don't go with other women at all—'

Bertha snorted. 'Spect me to believe that. I know what men are like.'

Eddie regarded her with pity and shook his head slowly. 'Bertha love, I wish you'd believe me. We're not all the same. Just because your dad was a ladies' man—'

'Don't you say things about my dad, Eddie Apple-yard. You're no saint.'

'The whole town knew about your dad and his carryings on, love.'

'I aren't sitting here listening to you calling my dad

names just to mek ya'sen feel better.' She wagged her finger in his face. 'He didn't get drunk and come home and knock his wife about.'

Appalled, Eddie stared at her. 'Bertha, I've never—'

'Oh 'aven't you? How do you know what you do when you're sow drunk?'

Eddie dropped his head into his hands. He couldn't believe it. He was not a violent man. Never had been. And though things were not right between him and his wife, he couldn't imagine that he would ever attack her physically. But then, he had to admit, he did get 'sow drunk' as the locals called it, a state that resembled a snoring, snorting pig. And, to his eternal shame, Eddie had to admit that he could not remember what he had done when he was in that state.

He couldn't even remember having brought the girl home from the town until Bertha pulled him from the trap and there the girl was, just sitting there. But that was something he was never going to admit. Not to his wife and certainly not to that poor lass. He didn't want her to think that he hadn't meant to help her, that he couldn't even remember making the offer.

'So?' Bertha was leaning towards him. 'What did happen to my pork pie and sausages?'

'It – it wasn't Tony,' Eddie stammered. 'It was me. I – I was hungry. In the night.' He wasn't used to telling lies. That was yet another thing he hadn't known he was capable of doing.

'If you expect me to believe that, Eddie Appleyard, you're even dafter than I thought you were.' She paused and her small, piercing eyes were boring into his soul. 'Is she still here? Is she still in the hayloft?'

Now he could answer honestly and even Bertha could detect the note of truth. 'No, she isn't.'

'Well, good riddance is all I can say. And if that's the truth, Eddie, then we'll say no more about it. And now I've got work to do even if you haven't.' She levered herself up and turned away, leaving her husband sitting at the table, his head still in his hands, vowing that as long as he lived he would never touch another drop of drink.

Four

From the scullery the boy heard his mother's chair scrape along the floor as she got up from the table. He scuttled out of the back door. He was halfway across the yard when the collie, chained up near its kennel, barked a greeting. The boy hesitated, glanced back towards the farmhouse and then hurriedly released the dog's collar from the chain.

'Come on then, boy.' Together they ran across the yard and out of the gate. In the gathering dusk the boy began to run up the track, the dog loping at his side. At the top of the hill Tony stopped to look down to where the cottage nestled against the trees. He could see a dim glow from the windows and knew that the girl was there.

He shivered, but whether from the cold or the misgiving he felt he could not be sure. Yesterday's rain had gone and stars shone in a clear sky, the moon a gleaming orb. There'd be a frost tonight. Though he was only ten, Tony knew about the weather and the changing seasons. He bent and pulled up his knee-length grey socks. He hadn't had time to change from his short school trousers. Nor had he stopped to put on his wellingtons. His mam'd scold if he messed up the leather lace-up boots he wore for school. He didn't want to make his mother cross with him. She seemed to spend a lot of the time cross these days, but mostly with his dad. The boy frowned and chewed on his lower lip. He couldn't understand why his mam and dad argued so much. But maybe all parents did. He didn't really know. He had some school pals whose homes he sometimes visited. He went to a birthday party now and then and one or two of the boys in his class had been to Cackle Hill Farm. But he still didn't know if other mams and dads carried on at each other like his did.

A gust of wind nibbled icily at his knees and his mind came back to the girl. *She'll be cold*, he thought. Without making any conscious decision, he began to walk slowly down the hill towards the cottage.

Anna had lit a fire from the kindling Eddie had brought her. Thoughtfully, he had also left a box of matches. She had drunk the milk and eaten most of the loaf of bread he had brought too. The hurricane lamp he had given her hung from a hook in the ceiling, casting eerie shadows around the walls.

'I'll bring you some more bits and pieces as soon as I can and I'll start work on the repairs tomorrow. I reckon the chimney'll need sweeping an' all.'

She'd looked him straight in the eye then. 'What about your wife? I don't want to bring trouble on you, Mister. You – you've been kind and I'd like to stay here for a few days. But maybe I'd better move on when I've rested a bit.'

'No.' His retort was swift and surprisingly firm. There was no way he was going to allow this girl to be turned away, especially not just before Christmas. 'No,' he said more gently. 'I – I want you to stay. Bertha needn't know. Not if we're careful. She never comes up this way. She never – ' there was a bitter tone to his words now – 'goes anywhere about the farm. The only time she goes out the house is to town. She dun't even use the village shop. Says she dun't want to give the gossips any more to chatter about. She – she dun't mix wi' folk easy.' He had smiled then, his eyes crinkling with a spark of mischief. 'But that's all to the good. She'll never know if I get things for you from the local shop, will she? And when I go into town next market day, I can get you some more bits of furniture.'

'Furniture? However are you going to get that past her?'

His smile broadened to a grin, his face looking suddenly years younger. 'I don't have to. The road to town runs yon side this wood and there's a track that comes round the other side of the trees to here and then on to our farm.' He gestured with his left hand in a vaguely northerly direction. 'We don't use this way, because the gate from our farm' – now with the other hand he pointed southwards – 'leads out onto the road between the town and the village.'

Anna could not hide the fear in her eyes. 'So – so does anyone use this track past the cottage?'

'Not many, love. Just farm workers now and again and mebbe – ' he chuckled suddenly – 'a poacher or two.'

She had dropped her gaze and breathed more easily.

And now, as the early darkness of a cold December evening came, she sat huddled against the fire. He had been right. The chimney did need sweeping, for every so often smoke puthered into the room, making her cough and her eyes smart. Once that was cleaned, she

29

would be able to build up the fire to use the bread oven, and when the holes in the walls and the roof were mended she could make this a very cosy little home.

If only ... Her thoughts started to drift but she shook herself physically and pulled herself back to the present.

It was then that she heard a scuffle outside the door from the kitchen and her whole being stiffened. It was too late to turn out the lamp and hide. She jumped at the soft tap on the door. She could not move, could not call out. She just sat there rigid with fear as, slowly, the door opened.

The boy stood framed against the darkness, blinking in the light from the lamp. They stared at one another for a moment and then the girl shivered in the frosty air coming into the room from the open door. The boy stepped inside and closed the door.

'I guessed you might be here. I came to see if you was all right. I – I thought you might be cold.'

She could see the man's features in the boy's face now; similar dark brown eyes and brown hair and a thin but well-shaped face. The boyish features would strengthen into a firm jawline and the father's kindness was already showing in the son's concern for her.

Anna summoned a smile. 'Does your dad know you've come up here?'

He shook his head. 'No.' He bit his lip and then blurted out, 'They're – they're rowing.'

Her smile faded. 'Over me?'

Tony shook his head. 'Not – not really. She thinks you've gone.' He moved closer and squatted down in front of the fire, holding out his hands to the meagre warmth the few sticks were giving. 'I'll get you some logs from the woods tomorrow before I go to school.'

'She doesn't know I'm here, then?' Anna asked softly.

He shook his head. He glanced up at her briefly and then looked back into the flames. Haltingly he said, 'I – don't reckon me dad wants her to know either.' Tony was reluctant to tell her that his father had lied to his mother over the food he had given the girl. He knew why his father had done so, but he wasn't happy about it. He felt torn between his parents. He didn't want his mam to be upset, yet he could understand why his father wanted to help this girl. What he couldn't understand was why his mother didn't want to help her too.

But Anna seemed to know, for she said quietly, 'No, I don't suppose he does.'

After a few moments Tony stood up. 'I'd better go. I've the hens to feed before I go to bed. It's one of me jobs,' he said importantly. 'And – and Mam might be looking for me.'

Anna nodded.

He hesitated a moment and then pulled a crumpled bar of chocolate from his pocket. Holding it out to her, he said, 'You can have this. It's mine. Me mam brought it for me from town. She won't know.'

Anna took it, unable to speak for the sudden lump in her throat. She had thought she had been past all feeling, past caring. Yet the actions of the farmer, and now his young son, made tears prickle behind her eyes.

'And I've brought someone to keep you company.'

For a brief moment her eyes were panic-stricken. 'I don't want . . .' she began, but already he had opened the door. In answer to his soft whistle a black and white collie trotted into the room and stood close to the boy, looking up at him with adoring, obedient eyes.

Tony fondled the dog's head. 'Stay, Rip. Stay here

31

with the lady.' He glanced up and smiled at her. 'He'll look after you.'

'Won't your mam miss him?' Anna asked, torn between wanting the animal's company and yet not wanting the boy's kindly action to bring him trouble.

Tony shrugged. 'She might, but I'm just hoping she won't.'

Anna tried to raise a smile, anxious to let him know that she appreciated his gesture.

'Thank you,' she said, her voice hoarse with gratitude. She held out her hand to the dog. The animal did not move until the boy nodded and said, 'Go on.' Then Rip padded across the floor and allowed himself to be patted by the stranger. He lay down on the floor and rested his nose on his paws, but his eyes once again sought his young master.

'Stay,' Tony said firmly and though, as the boy went out of the door, the dog gave a little whine, he did not move from his place beside Anna.

'Well, now,' she said softly, stroking the dog's head, 'it looks like we're both going to sleep here on the floor for the night.'

Wrapping herself in the horse blanket she had brought with her from the barn, she lay down between the dying fire and the dog. The animal's warm presence against her back soothed her chilled limbs and brought unexpected comfort to her lonely soul.

Five

The dog was scratching at the door, whining to be let out. Anna roused herself from heavy sleep and dragged herself up from the floor. She was stiff and cold. The fire had died out in the night and the room, never really warmed, was now freezing.

'All right, boy, I'm coming.' She opened the door and the dog ran out. She watched him streak up the hillside towards home. She closed the door and looked around the room in the pale light of early morning. There was little she could do except wait and see if the boy came as he had promised. What was his name? Tony, that was it. Maybe, later in the day, the man would come to see her too. Maybe he would bring her food. Maybe . . . Maybe . . .

She sighed, irritated to find herself dependent on these strangers for her survival. And she was afraid too. The man seemed kind, but why was he prepared to do so much for her? He was even risking trouble within his own family. Was he expecting something from her in return for his generosity? More than just helping him with the lambing? She shuddered and shied away from such thoughts. And how safe was this place anyway? The cottage was certainly isolated, nestling in a vale and obscured from the road by the wood. And it was on the farmer's land; that would offer some protection.

But was it enough?

It would have to be, she told herself. For now at least. If she rested here for a while, then, when she was feeling stronger, she could move on. Further away. She must get further away . . .

She heard a voice outside and looked out of the grimy window. She saw Tony with the dog bounding around him, leaping up to lick the boy's face. She could see that they were overjoyed to see each other again. The boy was laughing. 'Down, Rip, down. Good boy. Good dog.'

She opened the door and stood waiting until they reached her.

'I've come to get you some wood,' Tony said, smiling at her. 'Like I promised.' His face fell a little as he said, 'I'm sorry, but I couldn't get you anything to eat this morning. Me mam . . .' He fell silent, not wanting to sound disloyal to his mother, yet wanting to help the girl. 'Anyway, Dad's milking just now, but he gave me this to bring up. He'll be up later, he said, when he comes to the sheep.' The boy held out a can of milk.

'Thanks,' she said, taking the can eagerly and drinking thirstily.

'You're hungry, aren't you?' the boy said. 'I wish I could . . .'

'Don't worry,' she said at once. 'This is lovely. Really.'

There was a brief pause before he said awkwardly, 'I'd best get you the wood. I don't want me mam to miss me and it'll soon be school time.'

'I'll come with you and then I can find it for myself.'

He led the way in amongst the trees. The girl, still clutching the blanket around her, followed. The dog ran ahead, investigating the exciting smell of rabbit.

'I should have brought a sack,' Tony said, his arms soon full of twigs and broken branches.

'It's all right,' Anna said, taking off the blanket from around her shoulders. She shivered as she felt the loss of its warmth. 'We'll use this.' Together they collected enough kindling and larger pieces of wood to last her the day and carried their haul back to the cottage.

They tipped it onto the hearth and Tony squatted in front of the fireplace. He began to put the twigs into the grate. 'They're a bit damp. I don't think they'll catch light.'

'I'll see to it. You'd best be off.'

He stood up, for a moment feeling suddenly shy. 'Ta-ta, then.'

She nodded and managed a smile. 'Ta-ta,' she echoed.

'Come on, Rip.'

She watched them running up the track until they disappeared over the brow of the hill.

The boy had been right; the sticks were too damp to catch light and after the torrential rain she doubted there'd be anything in the woods that would be dry enough. And the dry kindling that Eddie had provided that first day was all gone. So, hugging the blanket around her again, Anna decided to look around the cottage. There just might be an old piece of wood she could use. There was nothing in the other room, where damp patches marked the floor and the wind whistled in through the broken windows. But when she climbed the ladder-like stairs and stepped into the two rooms under the roof, she found the floor littered with leaves that had blown in through a hole in the thatch and drifted into a corner. The leaves were brittle dry.

She filled the pockets of her coat and climbed down the ladder. Within minutes, the leaves caught light and she picked out the least wet of the twigs to pile on the top of the leaves. The fire smoked as before, but at least it was alight.

She drank the last of the milk and tended the fire. When she looked out of the window again, she was surprised to see that it was fully light, the winter sun pale in a watery sky. For a while she watched the sheep grazing on the slopes and then she saw the man coming down the track carrying a basket over one arm and two blankets under the other.

'Here we are then, lass,' he greeted her. 'I bet you're ready for this.' He held out the basket. There was bread, butter, cheese and more milk. 'Sorry it's not more. I'll go to the village shop later . . . Oh, you've got a fire going. That's good.'

'Your son came up earlier,' Anna said in her soft, husky voice. 'I hope you don't mind.'

Eddie pulled a wry expression. 'I don't. But if the wife finds out—'

'You – you'd better tell him not to come then. I don't want him getting into trouble on my account.'

The man shrugged. 'I don't reckon Bertha'll guess. He roams all over the farm with that dog of his. Gone for hours sometimes. Look,' he said, returning to the matter of her welfare, 'I'll mebbe manage to bring the tractor and trailer up this way later. I can't get into town until next market day without it looking odd, but I'll see what I can find in the outhouses. There's always bits and pieces we've thrown out.'

Later that day Eddie's tractor came chugging down the track with a loaded trailer behind him and pulled to a halt outside the cottage. To Anna, who had nothing, Eddie's barn seemed to have yielded a treasure trove.

'There's a kettle, a few old pots and pans and an armchair. It was me dad's.' His eyes clouded. 'Bertha threw it out the day after he died. And I've managed to get the old feather bed down from the loft when she was in the dairy,' he added, dragging it off the trailer. 'It'll be a bit damp. You'd better let it dry out before you use it.'

Remembering her soaking of two days earlier, Anna smiled to herself, but said nothing. She was hardly likely to take harm from a damp bed, she thought. But the man meant well.

Lastly he unloaded three sacks. 'There's potatoes from our own store and a few apples. And I've been to the shop for you. You'll have to let me know if I've forgotten anything you need.'

Anna stood, shaking her head in wonder. 'It's – it's wonderful. I don't know how to thank you.'

'No need, lass. You're working for me now, aren't ya?' He glanced at her and winked. 'And I always look after me employees.'

'I'll work for you, Mister. Oh, I'll work as hard as I can, but . . .' She touched the mound of her belly briefly.

He nodded sympathetically. 'Don't worry about that, lass. We'll cross that bridge when we come to it.'

But what would happen when they did come to that particular bridge, as he put it, even the man dared not contemplate. 'And now,' he said, trying to divert their thoughts. 'I must see to me sheep.'

'Can I help?'

'No, no, lass. You get ya'sen sorted out. And then – well – we'll see tomorrow, eh?'

Anna nodded. 'All right,' she agreed in her low, soft voice, 'but from tomorrow I want you to tell me what needs doing. And if you don't . . .' She smiled suddenly and the man stared at her, unable to take his eyes off her. She was a pretty lass, though a bit thin at the moment to his mind, but when she smiled her whole face seemed to light up. Even so, it was not enough to drive away the sadness in the depths of her dark eyes. 'And if you don't, Mister, then I'll *find* something.'

He laughed. 'Right you are then, lass. It's a deal.'

As he drove his tractor and trailer back towards the farm to fetch bales of hay for his sheep, Eddie was still smiling.

The following morning Anna walked across the meadow in front of the cottage towards the next field, where she could see the sheep contentedly munching long stalks of kale. She moved stealthily. Sheep were nervous creatures, easily panicked and bunching together in the face of danger and most of Eddie's ewes would be in lamb; the last thing she must do was to startle them.

Shading her eyes, Anna glanced round the edge of the field. There were several gaps in the hedges where the sheep could easily push their way into the neighbouring field. Anna began to smile. Here was something she could do to repay the farmer for his kindness. When the tractor and trailer chugged down the track later that morning, Anna was waiting for him.

'I don't suppose you've left those holes in the hedges for a reason, have you?'

'No, lass,' Eddie said wryly. 'I just haven't had time to repair them.'

'Right, then. You can bring me a billhook and a hedge knife too. Oh, and a few stakes.'

Eddie laughed. 'You're not going to try plashing, are you?'

Anna nodded.

Now he eyed her sceptically. 'Are you sure you can do it?'

Anna gave him one of her rare smiles. 'That's for you to say when I've had a go. I'll do one small gap first and then, if you're not satisfied, you can say so and I'll let well alone. All right?'

Eddie looked mesmerized. To him hedge-laying was a skilled art and one, he had to admit, that he had never been able to master properly.

Whilst he fetched the tools, Anna chose one of the smaller holes and began to clear the hedgerow of weeds and long, dead grass. By the time Eddie brought back the items she had asked for, Anna was ready to position two stakes in the gap. Then, taking up the billhook, she chose the thickest stem she could find in the existing hedge to the right of the hole and began to chip off all its side shoots.

'I'll – er – leave you to it, lass. I'll – um – come back later and see how you're getting on. Only don't tire ya'sen, will you?'

'I'll be fine, Mr Appleyard. It's nice to have something to do.'

Concern was still plainly written on the man's face, though whether it was for the pale waif who had come into his life or for his hedge, even Eddie could not have said. He glanced at her again and now his anxiety was wholly for her, but he was gratified to see a healthy pink tinge to her cheeks this morning. And the way she was wielding the billhook showed no sign of any ill effects from the cold night she must have spent in the cottage.

'I'll be off then,' he said again, still reluctant to leave his hedge. He sighed as he turned away. *Oh well*, he was thinking, *I don't suppose she can make a much worse mess of it than I would.*

A surprise awaited Eddie on his return to the field with Rip trotting beside him, pink tongue lolling, eyes ever watchful and alert. They stopped before the hole in the hedge – or at least where the hole had been. The thickest stems from the existing growth had been cut diagonally a few inches from the ground to a depth of about three-quarters of the thickness and bent carefully over so that the stem did not break. The branches then lay one above the other at angles of about thirty degrees across the gap in the hedge and were neatly woven in and out between the stakes. In time, new shoots from the old wood would form a thick hedge once more. Even the top had been neatly finished off.

Eddie stood gaping. He took off his cap, scratched his head and then pulled it on again, whilst Anna stood by, smiling quietly. 'By heck, lass, it's as good as I could do. No, if I'm honest, it's better. Where on earth did you learn to lay a hedge like that?'

Anna's smile faded and she turned away, but not before Eddie had seen tears fill her eyes.

'I had a good teacher, Mister,' she said huskily. 'A

40

very good teacher.' Then she took a deep breath and called to the dog. 'Come on, boy.'

As she bent to pick up her tools and move on to the next gap, Rip bounded alongside, leaving Eddie staring after her and then, glancing back to his newly repaired hedge, marvelling again at the young girl's workmanship.

Tony came each night after school to see her, always managing to bring something useful for her. And every night he ordered his dog to 'stay' with her.

'We've broke up from school today,' he told her near the end of the week following her arrival. 'It's Christmas next week.'

'Is it?' Anna said, surprise in her tone.

The boy stared at her. 'You hadn't forgotten?' he asked. To the boy, who had been counting the days, it was incredible that anyone could not know it was almost Christmas. Even his mam, who usually scorned merrymaking at other times, always loved Christmas. She had been mixing the puddings and baking mince pies all this last week. And last night she had helped him put up paper chains, looping them along the picture rail around the best parlour, which they would use on Christmas Day.

In answer to Tony's question, Anna shrugged. 'I've been travelling. I'd forgotten what date it is.'

'How long have you been travelling?' he asked with a boy's natural curiosity. 'Where d'you come from?'

Even the ten-year-old boy could not fail to notice the fear that sprang into her eyes at his question. She bit her lip and turned away. 'Oh, a long way away. You wouldn't know it.'

'I might,' he insisted. 'We've been doing geography at school on the British Isles and learning where lots of places are. I *might* know it.' He was trying to wheedle an answer from her, but now the girl said nothing and deliberately turned her back on him and his questions.

A few days before Christmas Tony brought her a hot mince pie. 'Me mam's just finished baking. She didn't notice I took an extra one.'

Anna bit into the light pastry with the warm juicy mincemeat inside. 'It's lovely,' she said. 'I wish I could send a message to your mam.' She smiled and suddenly some of the pain that was always in the depths of her violet eyes, lightened. 'But I'd better not.'

Tony was staring at her. 'You're ever so pretty when you smile,' he said with the innocent candour of a young boy. 'Haven't you got funny coloured eyes? I mean,' he added hastily, 'they're nice, but I've never seen anyone with eyes that colour before.'

At once the smile fled from her face and the anguish returned. Her words came haltingly, almost as if she were trying not to speak them, but an innate politeness was forcing her to do so. 'They're the same – colour as my – mother's.' The last word was spoken in a strangled whisper and, to the boy's horror, tears welled in her eyes.

'I'll be off,' he said gruffly, pushing his hands deep into the pockets of his coat. There was an embarrassed pause before he said, haltingly, 'I'll have to take Rip back with me tonight.'

He bit his lip. He didn't want to explain to the girl that there had been an awkward moment at home the previous evening. He had been sitting in his pyjamas in front of the kitchen range drinking cocoa when his mother, coming in from the outside privy, had said, 'Where's Rip? He's not chained up.'

Tony had felt his heart miss a beat and then begin to pound. He licked the line of chocolate from his upper lip and said, 'He – he wouldn't come home with me. He – he went off chasing rabbits, I think.'

'At this time of night? That's not like him. He's a very obedient dog usually. Specially with you, Tony. Oh well, mebbe it's not only rabbits he's chasing,' she added dryly. 'He's male, after all.'

Tony buried his nose in his mug to finish his drink. Then he stood up. Going to his mother, he put his arms around her and gave her an extra tight hug, trying to assuage his guilt at lying to her. 'Night, Mam.'

She had kissed his hair and patted his back. 'Night-night, love.'

Now, in the cottage, he commanded, 'Come on, Rip. Home, boy.'

The dog wagged his tail, but made no move to follow. Instead, Rip glanced at Anna and then sat down.

Tony slapped his own thigh. 'Come *on*, Rip.'

The dog flattened his ears and lay down, crawling on his belly, not towards his young master, but towards the girl.

Now it was the boy who had tears in his eyes. 'He's *my* dog,' he said. 'Not yours. I only lent him to you.'

'I know you did,' Anna said quietly, her own misery forgotten for the moment. 'Rip is confused, that's all.' She bent and stroked the dog's head and he licked her hand. 'Good dog. Go with your master now, boy. Go with Tony.'

As if understanding he had been released from any

43

obligation, Rip sprang up, barked and ran to the boy, leaping up to lick his face. Tony knelt and put his arms around the dog, hugging the wriggling body to him. Without another word, he turned and began to run up the hill, the dog racing ahead and then coming back to him.

Anna heard the boy's joyful laughter and the dog barking. As she closed the door against the dusk of approaching evening, she was already missing Rip's comforting presence in the cottage.

Six

Anna did not see the boy for the next three days, but each morning, when she opened the side door of the cottage to visit the privy, a small pile of wood was neatly stacked against the wall just outside. Later in the day Eddie would come to check on his sheep and would bring her food.

'All right, lass?' was his usual greeting and, as he left, he would say, 'Now, don't you go overdoing it, love.' It was the closest he ever came to referring to her advancing pregnancy.

Anna was surprised how much she missed seeing Tony, but there was plenty of work for her to do. She was kept busy collecting more wood to keep her fire burning through the cold nights and cleaning the inside of the one room in the cottage. She swept the floor and cleaned the windows and scrubbed out the bread oven. But, apart from the brief visits from Eddie and Rip, she saw no one. She had thought that solitude was what she wanted. She had believed she wanted to hide herself away from the world and all its cruelties, yet the farmer's kindness, and especially the boy's, had melted her resolve. Besides, she reminded herself, she had been desperate. Standing in the marketplace that night with nowhere to go, no money and hunger gnawing, she had known she could not hold out much longer.

If the man had not brought her to this place that

night, she doubted she would still have been alive by now. When she felt the child within her move, and in the moments of despair that still racked her, she wondered if it wouldn't have been for the best if she and the child had not survived. But the tranquillity of this place was already seeping into her wounded heart and bringing her a measure of peace. She was not happy – she doubted she would ever feel real happiness again – but she was no longer in the depths of misery. The instinct to survive was strong again within her. And now she had a place to stay. It was only when darkness closed in and she was alone in the cottage that the fear threatened to overwhelm her once more. Maybe she should ask Eddie for strong bolts for the two doors into the cottage. Perhaps then she would feel safe.

'I bet you thought I'd forgotten all about mending the walls,' Eddie called to her one afternoon, as he climbed down from his tractor and went to the trailer behind it to unload tools, wood and what looked suspiciously like a pile of wet mud.

Seeing her looking at it with a puzzled expression on her face, Eddie said, 'It's subsoil. I dug a hole ovver yonder near the stream. It's just right for this.'

Anna leant closer. 'What are all the bits in it?'

'Chopped-up pieces of barley straw. Now, all we need to do is mix it with a bit of sand and water and we'll be ready.' He smiled at her. 'Good, ain't it, when you can provide your own building materials? And it dun't cost me a penny,' he added, to reassure her that her presence in his cottage was not costing him a fortune.

Fascinated, Anna stood watching him nailing the

thin laths of wood into place and then plastering the mud mixture onto the wooden framework.

'I could do that,' she murmured, after watching him for a while.

He glanced up at her. 'Now, leave me summat to do, lass, else I shall start to feel I'm not needed.'

'Oh, you're needed, Mr Appleyard,' she murmured softly, thinking what might have happened to her by now if it hadn't been for this kind and generous man.

'Tell you what,' Eddie said. 'You'll be able to do the whitewashing when the mud's dried enough. How about that?'

By the time dusk came creeping across the field, the other downstairs room was already weatherproof.

'Joe Wainwright's promised to come early in the New Year to see to the roof,' Eddie said, straightening up to ease his aching back. 'That should make the upstairs rooms inhabitable if you should want to use them.'

Silently, Anna thought: *I won't be here by then*, but she did not want to seem ungrateful. Instead she asked, 'Do you think you could spare some whitewash for the inside walls? I hate asking for anything – you've been so good, but—'

'Course, lass. I should have thought of it mesen.'

'And – and could I have a snare? I could catch rabbits in the woods then.'

Now Eddie looked doubtful. 'I'm not too keen on setting traps or snares for wild creatures, love. I don't like to think of poor animals suffering, you know?' He pulled off his cap, scratched his head and then replaced his cap. Anna was beginning to notice that this was a habit with him when he was perplexed or anxious, or maybe even embarrassed in some way. 'Oh, I know I'm a farmer and I raise animals to be killed for meat, but that's done in a humane way.'

'I'm sorry,' Anna said swiftly. 'I shouldn't have asked.'

On Christmas Eve, in the late afternoon, there was a knock at the door. Anna's heart beat faster and her throat was dry as, standing in the shadows, she edged close to the window to see who was standing outside. When she saw the slight figure of the boy, she let out the breath she had been holding and opened the door with a genuine smile of welcome that widened when she saw the expression of apology on his face.

'I'm sorry,' he blurted out.

'Whatever for?' Anna said, pretending not to understand and, so that he would not have to explain his earlier childish petulance, she added swiftly, 'I know you can't come every day to see me.' She pulled the door wider, inviting him inside. 'But it's nice to see you when you can.'

She became aware that his coat was bulging, as if he was carrying something clutched to his chest.

'I've brought you a Christmas present,' he said.

'You shouldn't have . . .' Her voice faded away as she realized that the 'something' he carried was wriggling and pushing its way out from beneath his coat. A tiny wet nose appeared and then the silky black and white head of a collie puppy.

'Oh!' Reaching out with trembling hands, she whispered, 'For me? Is it really for me?'

The boy nodded, grinning broadly now, his earlier awkwardness forgotten. 'Me dad knows this farmer whose bitch had puppies a while back. It's all right. It's ready to leave its mother.' He handed the squirming creature to her.

Anna held the puppy against her breast and stroked its head, whilst it licked at her hand. 'Oh thank you, Tony, thank you,' she murmured. 'He's lovely.'

'You'll have to think of a name for him and when he's bigger you can train him to be a good sheep dog. Rip is,' he added proudly. 'Me dad trained him. He'd tell you what to do.'

For a brief moment, the girl's eyes clouded and seemed to take on a faraway look.

'What are you going to call him?'

Without even stopping to give thought to her choice, she said at once, 'Buster.'

'Buster,' the boy repeated, trying out the name aloud. Then he grinned and nodded. 'Yeah, it's a nice name. Buster. I'll bring you an old basket out of the barn tomorrow and—'

'It'll be Christmas Day. You mustn't come tomorrow. Your mam—' Her voice trailed away.

'Well, as soon as I can then.'

Rip was barking outside the cottage and the boy said, 'I'll have to be off.'

The puppy made all the difference to Anna. He demanded her constant attention and his antics brought the long-forgotten smile more readily to her mouth.

Tony landed with a thump on the end of his parents' double bed. 'Wake up. Wake up. It's Christmas Day.'

There were grunts and groans from both his mother and father.

'Whatever time is it?'

'It's not light yet. Go back to bed for a bit. There's a

49

good lad.' Eddie was burrowing further beneath the covers, trying to recapture sleep.

'But I want to open my presents.' A plaintive note crept into the boy's tone. 'Don't you want to see me open my presents?'

Bertha roused herself and threw back the covers. 'Course we do, love. Come on, Eddie, stir ya'sen. T'ain't Christmas every day.'

She pulled on her old dressing gown and pushed her feet into well-worn slippers. 'I just 'ope Father Christmas has remembered to bring me summat an' all.'

'Oh Mam,' Tony laughed. 'There isn't a Father Christmas.'

His mother pretended to look scandalized. 'What do you mean? Course there is. Who else do you think brings you all them presents? Enough to fill a pillow-case?'

Tony grinned and bounced up and down on the end of the bed. 'You do, Mam.'

'Well, I believe in Father Christmas,' she declared, her slippers flapping across the linoleum-covered floor. 'Not much else to believe in,' she muttered in a low voice so that the boy would not hear. 'Come on, then. Let's go an' see what he's left you.'

As the woman descended the stairs, grunting with each heavy tread, the boy scrambled to the top of the bed. 'Dad, Dad!' he whispered urgently. 'What about the girl? She'll be all alone. And it's Christmas. Are you going to see her today?'

Eddie yawned and stretched. 'I'll try, lad. But don't you go. Not today. Your mam'll want you to stay here today.'

'I took her the puppy. She – she was ever so pleased.

I could tell. She'd got tears in her eyes. But pleased tears. Not sad tears.'

'Had she, son?' The man put his hand on the boy's shoulder. 'I'm glad. The little chap'll be company for her, won't he?'

'Well, yes.' The boy was not convinced. 'But it's not the same as being with other people and having presents to open and a nice dinner and . . .' His voice trailed away as he thought about their own day ahead here in the cosy farmhouse. It was a stark contrast to the draughty cottage and the meagre fare that Anna would be facing.

Eddie patted his son's shoulder again and said, 'Run along. I'll be down in a minute. I'll see what I can do later.'

The next few hours were spent happily. Even Bertha was delighted with the gift that Eddie had bought her, a warm dressing gown and cosy slippers. Luckily, she couldn't know that, as she slipped them on and paraded around the parlour, his thoughts were not on her, but with the lonely girl in the cottage over the hill. Hidden in the barn were some clothes for her. Useful, serviceable clothes and not new, but his desire to see her face when he presented them to her, the delight he hoped to see in her expression was in the forefront of his mind. But he played the part of dutiful husband and doting father. The latter was not difficult, for Tony's pleasure in the day was obvious and even Bertha had gone to a lot of trouble over the Christmas dinner. Goose and all the trimmings followed by Christmas pudding and brandy sauce.

But all the time he was eating it, Eddie was wondering how he could take some to the girl. He didn't guess

51

that, as they sat side by side at the table, his son was worrying about exactly the same thing.

In the afternoon Tony played with his new toys whilst Eddie helped Bertha wash up. It was the only day in the year when he lent a hand in the kitchen.

'You've spent your morning cooking for us, love,' he always said. 'It's only fair I give you a hand to clear up. Not much of a Christmas Day for you otherwise, is it?'

Later, as Bertha played a noisy game of Snap with Tony, Eddie said, 'I'd better nip out and check the animals. Feed Duke and Rip. I reckon they deserve a Christmas dinner an' all.'

'There's some scraps on the side for the dog,' Bertha said absently and then shouted loudly, 'SNAP! You missed that one, Tony. You weren't watching.'

'Sorry, Mam,' the boy mumbled and looked down again at the cards, but not before he and his father had exchanged a meaningful glance.

This time it was Tony who shouted loudly, 'SNAP!' Now he was happy to pay full attention to the game for he knew from the look that his father was going to take a plateful of Christmas dinner to the girl.

Seven

In January the weekly ration of fresh meat for each person was cut yet further. And there were gloomy predictions that there would soon be a cut in the bread ration, with no hope of any increase either in eggs, bacon or fish.

'You'd've thought they'd be increasing rations now, not cutting 'em further,' Bertha grumbled. 'The war's been over two years come May.'

But Eddie was more philosophical. 'That's one advantage of living on a farm,' he told Anna later and winked conspiratorially as he smuggled more food to her without Bertha knowing. 'Always a bit extra for us that no one need know about.'

The girl was staring at him, a stricken look in her violet eyes.

'I'm sorry, lass,' Eddie said hastily. 'I didn't mean to worry you.'

As she turned from him, she lifted her hand in a gesture of reassurance. 'It's all right. It's just . . .' But she did not finish her sentence and moved away, leaving Eddie staring after her with a puzzled expression. He waited for her to turn back again, to say more, but no explanation was forthcoming.

What on earth could he possibly have said to make that look of fear leap into her eyes once more?

Eddie sighed. The lass was a mystery and no mistake.

Towards the end of January, freezing weather gripped the whole country in its icy fingers. Power failures plunged towns and villages into darkness, whilst the temperature dropped lower and lower.

Cackle Hill Farm had its own generator, but Eddie was concerned for the girl in the cottage. Every few days he took a bag of coal with him on his trailer, hidden beneath the feed for his sheep.

Anna looked out of the cottage one morning to see a slate grey sky. She lifted her face and sniffed the air. *Snow*, she thought. *There's snow coming and a lot of it.*

'How many sheep have you got?' she asked Eddie later when he came on the tractor with bales of hay for his flock.

'About fifty. Why?'

'I reckon we're in for some snow, Mr Appleyard.'

Eddie glanced at the laden sky and then at the girl. 'Aye,' he agreed, marvelling at her knowledge. 'I was thinking the same mesen.' Just who was this girl, he was wondering, and where had she come from? She was certainly knowledgeable about the countryside and about farming. The image of her hedge-laying was in his mind. She was looking about her now, glancing over the sheep, which were grazing with placid contentment unaware of the threatening weather. Eddie was sure that the girl was thinking the same thing he was – his flock ought to be under cover before the snow came. It was the most animated he had seen her, the most conversation they had had. Even over the hedging, she had not been quite so interested, so concerned, so – alive!

He smiled, thankful to see the change in her. 'Call me "Eddie". Everyone does. Meks me feel old to be called "Mester Appleyard".' For a brief moment she looked uncertain, as if, suddenly, her growing trust in him had been threatened. He saw her glance at him and he couldn't mistake the suspicion in her eyes. And something else too. Could it possibly be fear? Hastily, he added, 'Only if you want to, of course. Mebbe I ought to call you "Miss Woods". But to hear mesen called "Mester Appleyard",' he went on, trying to make a joke of it, 'meks me think me dad's come back.'

Her expression lightened a little and there was even the ghost of a smile as she said softly, 'No, no. "Anna" is just fine . . .' There was a long pause before she added almost inaudibly, 'Eddie.'

'Now, about these sheep,' Eddie said, deliberately changing the subject, his gaze roaming over the nearby slopes, 'we could be in real trouble if the snow comes. We're due to start lambing any time.'

Horrified, Anna stared at him. 'As early as this?'

Eddie nodded. 'I usually plan it to start in February, with a batch of about twenty.' He tapped the side of his nose. 'Then I can get them to market by late June or early July when the prices are good. The rest lamb in March and April. Those lambs get the clean grazing, the new grass that year. Then I can sell them any time I want or keep a few to add to my own flock.'

Anna smiled and began to say, 'That's what—'. She stopped and bit her lip. Sensing her thoughts were again turning to a troubled past, Eddie tactfully hurried on. 'They lamb outdoors unless the weather's bad, then, I take them down to the barn. But as soon as the lambs are strong enough, I bring 'em back to the field.' He paused and then laughed wryly. 'Course, some of 'em are awk'ard beggars and drop too early. That's when we end up in your cottage.'

'It must be a busy time for you,' she murmured, her eyes still with a faraway look.

'Tony helps when he can.' He laughed. 'I forget sometimes just how young he is. He's a good lad.'

'Mm, I can see that,' Anna murmured. She did not ask if Bertha ever helped for she'd guessed the answer.

'Mebbe' – Eddie was glancing worriedly at the sky and thinking out loud – 'I ought to get as many as I can of the flock down to the yard. I can't get all fifty under cover, but at least they'd all be in one place.'

'It'd certainly be better than them getting buried in the snow out here. We'd never find them. And when those that are due start lambing—'

'I'll bring Rip and Tony up tomorrow and we'll start rounding them up. One day off school won't matter.'

'There's no need to keep him off. I can help you.'

Eddie nodded. 'All right then, lass. I'll see you bright and early in the morning.'

'Eddie,' she said suddenly, as he began to climb back onto his tractor, 'leave me your crook, will you?'

He eyed her speculatively. 'Course I will. But what do you want with it? I mean, you didn't ought to be tugging about with sheep. Not in your . . .' His voice trailed away, but when he glanced briefly towards her stomach she understood. 'Now, promise me you won't.'

Touched by his concern, she smiled, though as always the smile scarcely reached her eyes. The deep sadness in them was something that haunted Eddie Appleyard even when he was not with her.

'I'd just feel better if I had one,' she answered, neatly

evading giving her promise and knowing he would not deny her request.

Eddie reached into the trailer behind his tractor and handed her his shepherd's crook.

'This isn't your only one, is it?' she asked softly, running her hands lovingly up and down the polished wood.

He laughed. 'Lord, no. I've two more and Tony's even got his own little one. I had it specially made for him.'

Anna closed her eyes and sighed, and when she opened them again Eddie was startled to see tears brimming. Her voice was husky as she said, 'That's nice.' Then swiftly, she turned away.

As he drove up the track, Eddie was filled with acute sadness, yet he didn't quite know why. Every so often something was said or something happened that seemed to remind the lass of her past – something that brought tears. He wished she would open up, that she would tell him more about herself. He sighed. There was nothing more he could do except look after her – no matter what it cost him.

As he drove into the yard and climbed down from his tractor, he saw Bertha standing in the doorway, her arms folded across her bosom. Scowling, she shouted, 'And what's so interesting up yon track, might I ask?'

As he walked towards her, he forced a smile. 'Me sheep,' he said and added mildly, 'Any tea in the pot, Bertha love?'

The snow came that night. It began stealthily, falling innocently enough at first and clothing the world in a thin, white sheet.

The following morning Eddie, Anna and Rip rounded up thirty-three sheep and drove them down to the farmyard, though Anna was careful to stay out of sight of the house. Another ten wandered down to the cottage of their own accord and sheltered near the walls or beneath the trees. By dinnertime the snow was coming thick and fast.

'There's still seven missing,' Anna panted, leaning on her crook and screwing her eyes up against the huge flakes that settled on her face. They clung to her hair and covered her shoulders.

'You go in now, love. You're beginning to look like a walking snowman. You'll be soaked through.' He didn't refer to the day he had found her and brought her home, yet it was in both their minds. She had changed even in that short time. Now she had a home, she was warm and well fed. Now she was able to laugh and retort, 'So do you.'

Beside them, Rip shook himself vigorously, the snow from his coat showering them both with even more.

'We must find them,' Anna insisted as her thoughts returned to the missing animals.

'Me an' Rip'll keep looking, but it's pretty hopeless in this lot. We can't see more than a few yards in front of our noses, never mind trying to see sheep across the field. If it'd only stop snowing, we might have a better chance.'

'But seven,' Anna said, 'that's a lot to lose.'

'I know,' Eddie said soberly, 'but think of all those we've saved. Besides, they might be all right if it stops soon.'

They both glanced at the sky and then at each other, but neither spoke. They didn't need to. The sky was so heavy with snow that it was almost like the dusk of evening even though it was only midday. They both knew that the snow would keep coming until it was ankle deep, then up to the knee and, finally, almost too deep for anyone to wade through. They were facing day after day of blizzards that would shroud the countryside and bring transport, movement of any kind, to a halt. The lanes and then the roads would soon be impassable and only tractors or vehicles with heavy chains on their wheels would be able to move anywhere. Children from outlying areas would not get into the village school. Isolated farms and houses would be snowed in and would have to rely on their own food stores.

That first evening, when Eddie returned, wet through, aching in every limb and disconsolate because he had not found even one of his missing sheep, Bertha was already fretting. 'I'm going to be trapped 'ere, not knowing if me sister's alive or dead.'

'I'll take you into the town on the tractor, love, if it gets that bad and you're worried about her,' Eddie offered.

His wife's retort was scathing. 'Spect me to ride on that thing? I'd be a laughing stock.'

'Nobody's laughing, Bertha. We'll have to get about as best we can.'

'Aye well, you're all right, aren't you? You can still get into town of a Wednesday.' She leant towards him, wagging her finger. 'Only thing is, Eddie Appleyard, you can't drink like a fish no more, 'cos the tractor won't know it's own way home like that poor old pony.'

Eddie turned away without replying. There was no talking to the woman sometimes. He couldn't believe that she had not noticed by now – and he certainly wasn't going to remind her – that he had not come home drunk, not once, since the night he'd brought the girl home. He had kept his silent vow of abstinence, but Bertha hadn't even commented on it.

In the cottage, Anna didn't mind the weather. In fact, it made her feel more secure. No one could reach her now. No one would find her hidden away in a snow-covered cottage near the wood. And she had all the supplies she needed. In the weeks since Christmas she had built up a woodpile in the next room and, thanks to Eddie, she had a good store of tinned food in the larder. She and the puppy would be fine – the only thing that concerned her was Eddie's sheep.

Gently, young though he was, Anna had begun to train the puppy. She would whistle softly in different tones and different pitches and repeat the words of instruction that the shepherds used. When he grew bigger and spring came, then she would take him into the fields and teach him properly.

But sometimes the tears overcame her and she buried her face in his soft coat, remembering that other dog called Buster who had been hers in that other life.

The following morning Anna looked out to see a white world outside her window. But, for the moment, the snow had stopped falling. After a hasty breakfast, she pulled on her warmest clothes and the wellingtons Eddie had brought her.

'Now you stay here, warm and cosy by the fire,' she said to little Buster, who, sensing that he was going to be left alone, whimpered. 'It's a pity you're not bigger like . . .' she began and then faltered, blinking back sudden tears. Then she added bravely, 'You could be a great help today.'

With a final pat, she opened the front door. Normally, she used the door from the kitchen, but today she had another idea. At once a deluge of snow that had drifted against it during the night fell in and it took the girl several precious minutes before she could get the door closed again and then begin to dig a path away from the cottage.

'This is worse than I thought,' she muttered, resting on her spade for a moment. Digging away the snow was hard work and the ever-increasing bulge of her stomach hampered her. But the thought of the sheep buried out there in the fields spurred her on. 'Worst of it is,' she muttered to herself, 'they're such silly creatures. They might not be together. They could be anywhere.' But her words were spoken fondly. She had a great affection for sheep and it was this that was making her disregard her own safety – even the well-being of her unborn child – in an effort to save the rest of Eddie Appleyard's flock.

First, she dug her way round to the back of the cottage, to find the sheep huddled against the back wall of the cottage, their long coats matted with snow.

'You poor things, you do look miserable. Come on, let's get you in the warm.' Grabbing hold of the nearest one, she began to lead it round the side of the building and in through the front door and pushed it into the empty 'parlour' of the cottage. Two had followed her of their own accord and, with three similar trips, she soon had all the sheep under cover. She counted them. Ten. Yes, she had been right. Somewhere on the snow-covered hills were seven more. Already the little room looked crowded, but Anna was determined to find the others and bring them to safety.

'Now for the difficult bit,' she murmured, taking up the crook and plodding round to the front of the cottage.

Snow was falling again, but only light, small flakes. Even though the sky looked laden, at the moment she could still see across the fields. Anna scanned the slopes. Taking a deep breath, she pushed her way through the deep snow towards the side of the field. Sheep tended to look for shelter and when the snow began the hedgerows would be the most likely place to find them.

She had unearthed two by the time she heard a shout and looked up to see Eddie, Tony and Rip struggling to reach her.

'I thought – you promised me . . .' Eddie panted as he neared her, 'that you wouldn't do this.'

For the first time Anna laughed aloud throwing back her head, the joyous sound echoing around them. For a moment, Eddie and Tony stood looking at her and then, unable to stop themselves, they laughed too.

Anna was shaking her head. 'I didn't actually answer you.' Then she looked at him with an expression that was almost coy. 'But I expect you're used to being obeyed.' And she nodded towards Tony.

Eddie smiled, but there was a wry twist to his mouth now. 'By Tony, yes. Well, most of the time.'

He looked at the two bedraggled sheep standing miserably in the snow. 'I'm surprised they're still alive.'

'Luckily, they weren't buried very deep, but we'd better get on looking for the rest . . .'

'Oh no! You're doing no more. You take this pair back to the cottage and . . .'

Her face was suddenly mutinous. She shook her head. 'Not until we've found the others.'

The man and the young girl stared at each other, whilst the boy looked from one to the other, watching the battle of wills between them.

'You need my help,' Anna said, her expression softening. 'Let me repay you for your kindness when I can. Please?'

He sighed. She was right. He did need her help, but he was worried about her. Even in the short time he had known her, her belly had swelled. She couldn't have much longer to go, he thought.

'Well,' he said still doubtful, but weakening. 'All right, but promise if you feel tired you'll stop.'

'Yes, I'll promise you that.'

'Right. Tony, you take these two down to the cottage . . .' Eddie said and Anna added, 'In through the front door and into the other room. The one to the left.'

Eddie stared at her. 'You've got some inside?'

She nodded. 'The ones that were sheltering at the back of the cottage.' She laughed. 'They're guests in my front parlour now.'

They worked – the three of them – until late afternoon, until all but one sheep had been accounted for.

'We'll have to leave it at that. I'll take these down to the yard if they can make it through the snow. Mebbe she'll turn up.' Eddie's thoughts were still with his one lost sheep. 'Mebbe she's wandered off and found her own shelter somewhere.' But his tone was not convincing.

'I wanted to find them all,' Anna murmured, her gaze still roaming the hillsides, but in the gathering dusk she could no longer see very far.

'We've found more than I dared to hope thanks to you, lass,' Eddie said. 'Can you manage with those twelve? I really can't get any more into the barn.'

'It's a bit crowded, but yes. They'll be fine.'

'I'll bring some feed for them, but now into the cottage with you and get yourself dry and warm.'

'I will, but first . . .' Letting her crook fall, Anna bent and scooped up a handful of snow. Then she moulded it into a ball. 'Let's have snowball fight.' And she lobbed the ball of snow at Tony, catching him full in the chest.

For a brief moment, the man and the boy stared at her in amazement. Then, with a whoop they began to fling snow at her and at each other until a blizzard of snowballs was flying through the air and their laughter was echoing through the dusk and the gently falling snowflakes.

At last, breathless, they stopped, bending over to catch their breath. As she straightened up, Anna's laughter turned into a cry as pain stabbed at her stomach and she fell to her knees in the snow.

'What is it?'

She was bending double, crouching in the snow and groaning. 'It – hurts,' she gasped.

'Let's get you inside. Then I'll have to fetch the midwife from the village. I reckon it's your bairn coming, lass.'

She clutched his arm and looked up at him with terrified eyes. 'No – no. I don't want anyone else here. And I don't want the baby.' Her voice rose to a hysterical pitch as she gripped Eddie's arm with an intensity that frightened him. 'I won't have it. I won't.'

Eight

They helped her back to the cottage. The man was worried and the young boy's eyes were wide and fearful. All Tony wanted to do was to run as far away as possible.

'Let's get you into the warm and lying down,' Eddie said, aware of how inadequate warmth and comfort were in the snowbound, isolated cottage.

'Shall I go and get Mam?' Tony asked.

'No,' the girl cried. 'No. I don't want anyone.'

As another spasm of pain gripped her, she grasped Eddie. 'I don't want anyone else. Promise me. I don't want anyone to know I'm even here.'

He didn't answer her, but pushed open the door and half carried her inside the cottage. 'Lie down,' he commanded. His voice was gentle, but there was a note of firmness in his tone. 'Now, look here, lass. I respect your feelings. Whatever reason you've got, I know you don't want other folks around. But this is different. I can't manage on me own . . .'

'Why not? You know about sheep – about lambing . . . aah . . .' Her words ended in a cry of pain and she held her stomach.

Eddie could not help a wry smile. 'This is a bit different, love, than helping a few lambs into the world.'

'I don't see why,' she panted, as the contraction faded.

Eddie shook his head. 'I'm going to the village to fetch the midwife. I'll ask her not to say owt. Pat Jessop's a good sort.' His face sobered. 'I'd never forgive mesen, if owt happened to you – or to the bairn.'

Anna closed her eyes as she whispered dully, 'It wouldn't matter. It wouldn't matter to anyone. Maybe it'd be for the best.'

Eddie took her hand and squeezed it. 'Don't say things like that, lass. It'd matter to me. To both of us.' He turned and looked at his son. 'Wouldn't it, Tony?'

The boy nodded. He was still frightened. He'd seen lambs and calves born all his young life. But, like his dad said, this was very different. At his father's next words his fears increased.

'Now, son, you stay here with Anna while I go back to the farm and fetch the tractor. I'm going to tell your mam that I've got to stay up here with the sheep. Then I'll go to the village and fetch Mrs Jessop and when I get back with her, you can go home.'

Seeing the boy's terror, Eddie put his hand on Tony's shoulder. 'Don't leave her, lad. I'm counting on you. I won't be long.'

The boy's voice trembled as he asked, 'What if Mam comes looking for me?' He put out his hand to fondle his dog's head. Rip had come to sit beside his young master, his attention divided between Tony and the boisterous puppy. Buster was leaping around him, giving excited little yelps, inviting the older dog to play. But Rip sat obediently to heel.

'She won't,' Eddie replied, trying to sound more confident than he felt. Bertha would never venture out to look for her husband, but Tony was a different matter. She just might be worried enough about him to brave the weather.

'Please, oh please, don't go,' Anna moaned, but Eddie was adamant. 'I have to, lass.'

'But it's coming. It's coming.' Her voice rose in anguish.

'No, it isn't. If I know owt about these things, you're going to be a while yet. Specially . . .' He had been going to add 'with your first', but he thought better of it. Instead, he patted her hand encouragingly and turned away. 'I'll be as quick as I can.'

He trudged back through the snow to the farmhouse.

'Where's Tony?' was Bertha's first question.

'He's all right.' Eddie managed to sound convincing and, as much as he could, he determined to keep to the truth. His lies would sound more convincing. 'We've got all the remaining sheep into the cottage, bar one. And one or two of them look as if they're going to start.' If only she knew just who it was that was 'lambing', he thought wryly. 'I'll have to stay up there for a bit, love. I've come for the tractor. I – I need some bits and pieces from the village. Anything you want while I'm going?' he added swiftly, hoping to divert her from asking too many questions about what was happening in the fields.

'No, no, I don't think so,' Bertha said abstractedly, then, returning to her main cause for concern, she added, 'You're not to keep Tony up there all night.'

'No, no, love, of course not. I'll make sure he comes home well before dark. But,' he added, with more truth than she could ever know, 'I know he's only young, but he's a great help to me.'

'You don't have to tell me that,' Bertha said and there was pride in her tone. For a moment she softened. 'You get off to the village and I'll pack you some food up now and you can call for it on your way back.'

Eddie swallowed, feeling trapped. He hadn't planned on coming back this way, but on taking Mrs Jessop further along the lane and in by the track round the far side of the woods to reach the cottage. He couldn't risk Bertha seeing Pat Jessop riding on his tractor complete with her midwife's bag. But all he could say was, 'Righto, love. That'd be grand.'

As he rode into town on his tractor, Eddie worked out a plan. *I'll take Pat straight to the cottage, then double back round by the lane and into the farmyard. That way I can collect what she's packed up for me and then go back up the track from the farm to the cottage.* It was lucky, he thought, that the lane was not visible from the farmhouse. Bertha wouldn't be able to see him going past the gate and then coming back again. Not unless she was out in the yard near the gate. And he very much doubted she would be. Not in this weather! He smiled to himself, beginning to enjoy the intrigue.

'Who'd have thought it?' he muttered aloud. 'Quiet old Eddie Appleyard having a bit of excitement in his life.'

Left in the cottage with Anna and the two dogs and with twelve sheep now huddled in the next room, Tony was mentally counting the seconds from the moment his father left.

'Can I – get you anything?' he asked tentatively.

Anna, lying quietly for the moment, with her eyes closed, shook her head. 'I'm sorry,' she said, 'that you're having to see this. You shouldn't be here.'

Tony shrugged, suddenly feeling important. 'S'all

right. I've seen lambs and calves an' that born. I know
all about it.'

Anna smiled weakly. Did he? Did he really know the
whole process? How a lamb, a calf, a child was con-
ceived? Perhaps he did, she thought. He lived on a farm.
Had done all his young life. He must have seen the ram
in the fields with the sheep, the bull with the cows and
maybe Eddie even allowed him to watch when the boar
visited. For an intelligent boy it wouldn't be too great
a step to imagine what happened between a man and a
woman . . .

Anna groaned and covered her face with her hands,
trying to keep the memories at bay.

'Is it hurting again?' Tony asked.

She let out a deep sigh and tried to relax her body.
'Not just now.'

But only a minute later she was doubled up again
and thrashing about the bed in agony. Tony backed
away from her, standing pressed against the far wall,
wanting to run, but knowing that he could not, must
not, leave her.

He had promised his dad.

Rip whined and pressed against the boy's legs. Even
the puppy's lively scampering was quietened. Giving
little whimpering cries, he nestled between Rip's paws.

If only, Tony agonized, she would stop crying out in
pain.

Eddie banged loudly on the door of the village midwife's little cottage. Wintersby village was lucky to have
a trained district nurse cum midwife living there. Not
all villages had one and a trip to the market town of

Ludthorpe would have been impossibly slow in this weather, even on the tractor.

The door was flung open and the tall, buxom figure of Pat Jessop stood there.

'Eddie.' She smiled in welcome. 'What brings you here? Something wrong, ducky?'

'I need your help, Pat.' At her gesture of invitation, he knocked the snow from his boots and stepped inside the door. As she closed it, he pulled off his cap.

'Slip your boots off and come into the kitchen. Tell me all about it,' she said leading the way.

Eddie and Pat Jessop, Pat Anderson as she had been then, had attended the village school at the same time. They had played together as children and Pat had loved nothing better than visiting Cackle Hill Farm and helping with the harvest or, as she had grown older, lambing time. She always said it had been that experience that had led her into nursing. Yet, because she had gone to train in the hospital on the hill in Ludthorpe and had lived in the nurses' home there, the tender romance that might have blossomed between her and Eddie had withered. Pat had fallen in love with a handsome night porter on the hospital staff and, eventually, Eddie had married Bertha. Pat's husband had been killed in the recent war and sadly there had been no child from the union for Pat to love and cherish in his memory. Her loving nature could now only find fulfilment in the care of her patients and nothing gave her greater joy than bringing a child safely into the world.

'I've a bit of trouble on, Pat.' Eddie stood awkwardly in the tiny kitchen, turning his cap through restless fingers.

'Sit down, Eddie, and have a cup of tea.'

'I'd love to, Pat, but I can't stay. I need your help.'

Swiftly, he explained how he had met Anna and taken her home with him. 'Bertha doesn't know she's staying in me cottage. And,' he added pointedly, 'she mustn't.'

'Oh, Eddie,' she murmured, shaking her head at him in gentle admonishment, 'you and that big heart of yours. It'll get you into real trouble one of these days.'

With wry humour, Eddie ran his hand through his hair. 'I think it already has, Pat.'

Pat pulled a face. 'I have heard the tittle-tattle in the village. Not that I take any notice of it,' she added swiftly, 'or repeat it.'

'I know you wouldn't, Pat,' Eddie said softly.

'Anyway, right now we must think about this girl. You think she's gone into labour, Eddie?'

'I'm sure of it.'

'Just give me five minutes to put me warmest clothes on and get a few things together and I'll be with you.'

It had begun to snow again as they started on the journey back to the farm, which lay about a mile outside the village. Pat, muffled in a mackintosh, scarves and wellingtons, sat on the mudguard over the huge back wheel of the tractor. She had dispensed with her official district nurse's uniform in favour of slacks and jumpers. She knew just how long this night might be.

Dusk was closing in as they reached the cottage, to see Tony standing in the doorway. There were tears running down the boy's face and as soon as the tractor stopped and Eddie and Pat climbed down, he ran towards them and flung himself against his father.

'Come quick. She's screaming and screaming all the time now and – and there's water and blood too—'

'Oh my God!' Eddie muttered, but already Pat was hurrying into the cottage.

'Now, ducky, here I am. You'll be all right. Let's have a look at you.'

The man and the boy stood in the shadows, feeling helpless but unable to tear themselves away.

Anna was bathed in sweat and clutching the sides of the mattress. She was crying out and writhing in agony.

'Now, now, calm down. I'm here now and everything will be all right,' Pat was saying, soothing the terrified, pain-racked young girl. Pat examined her swiftly and looked up, smiling. 'It's only your waters broken, ducky. Everything's just fine. Baby will be fine. Now, when's your due date?'

The girl's head moved from side to side.

'When did the doctor tell you your baby would come, ducky?' Pat persisted gently.

'Never – seen – a doctor,' Anna gasped. 'I don't want it.' Her voice rose. 'I don't want it.'

Briefly, Pat left Anna's side and crossed the small room to Eddie.

'This isn't going to be easy,' she whispered. 'She's fighting it. Send the boy home, but you'll have to stay, Eddie. I'll need you. Get that fire built up. Plenty of hot water and—' Her eyes fell on the two dogs in the corner. She pointed in horror. 'And get them out of here this minute.' At that moment bleating came from the next room and Pat's eyes widened. 'Oh, Eddie, don't tell me! You've got sheep in there, haven't you?'

Eddie nodded.

Pat sighed and shook her head. 'Eddie Appleyard, what am I to do with you? This is hardly the ideal place anyway for the lass to give birth, but with animals a few feet away . . . I don't want her getting an infection.

So,' she went on, rolling up her sleeves, 'get me a bowl of hot water and the first thing we'll do is wash in disinfectant. Both of us. Where's my bag? Ah, there it is.' As she turned she added, 'You still here, Tony? Off you go and take those dogs with you.'

Tony cast a wide-eyed glance at his father. 'I can't take Buster home. What'll Mam say?'

'Put him in with Duke. She never goes in there.'

Tony picked up the puppy. Like his father, he knew that Bertha never went anywhere near the pony unless it was safely harnessed between the shafts of the trap. Buster made little yelping noises and licked the boy's face, ecstatic to be fussed.

'Have I time to take the tractor back and pick up some food? Bertha was packing summat up for me. I – I don't want her to wonder why I haven't gone back.'

Pat could only guess at the full story from the brief outline Eddie had given her, but, knowing his wife, she realized the importance of Eddie's request. 'Yes, go on, but be as quick as you can.'

Eddie put his hand on his son's shoulder. 'You run on home, son, but not a word to your mam.'

The boy nodded and turned towards the door, but before he left he gave one last glance at the girl on the bed. Then he was out of the door and wading through the snow as fast as he could. As he went, he heard Anna's last, despairing cry. 'I don't want it. Let me die. Just let me die.'

Nine

The birth itself was straightforward enough. The baby was small, a little early, Pat thought, but it was the girl's attitude that concerned her. Anna screamed and writhed, fighting the pain.

'When you get a contraction, you've got to push,' Pat told her, but irrationally Anna would only shout, 'I don't want it. I don't want it.'

Kindly, but firmly, Pat said, 'Well, you can't leave it in there, ducky.'

Eddie kept the fire built up and soon the room was hot and stifling. He fetched and carried to Pat's commands and, as she brought the child, kicking and screaming, into the world, he was standing beside her, holding Anna's hand and mopping the girl's brow gently.

'You've a lovely baby girl, Anna. She looks a bit premature, but she's beautiful and what a pair of lungs!' Pat laughed and held up the wriggling infant. Swiftly, she wrapped the baby in a piece of flannelette sheeting. 'I'll see to you in a minute, my pet,' she murmured. 'Here, Eddie, you'll have to hold her for a moment. I must get the placenta.'

'Me?' Eddie looked startled.

'Yes, you, Eddie Appleyard. I don't see anyone else handy.'

Eddie sat down in the battered old armchair he had

brought from his barn for Anna and held out his arms. Gently, Pat laid the tiny infant in the crook of his elbow and watched Eddie's face soften as he looked down at the baby girl. If Pat Jessop had not known Eddie so well that she believed every word he had told her implicitly, at that moment she could have believed that the child was indeed his. Watching his tender expression and the gentle way he held the child, as if she were the most precious being on God's earth, brought a lump to Pat's throat. There were going to be plenty of the village gossips who would believe that he was the father once this news got out. But no one would hear it from Nurse Jessop.

'Now then,' she said briskly, turning back to the new mother, who was lying quietly with her eyes closed. Anna's cheeks were red with the effort of giving birth, but it was not the colour of robust health. The young girl was very thin and Pat wondered if she would have enough milk to feed the child naturally.

'Now, Anna, you're lucky you don't need any stitches, but we've got to get the afterbirth away. I'll have to massage your tummy.' Drowsily, the girl opened her eyes and frowned. 'That hurts.'

'Sorry, love, but I have to do it.' When that did not produce the desired effect, Pat said, 'Can you cough, ducky?'

Anna made a little noise in her throat.

'Come on, Anna. A real good, deep cough. Right from your boots. That's it. Good girl,' Pat exclaimed as the placenta came slithering out. 'That's what I wanted. Now we'll get you cleaned up and you can rest while I wash the baby. Then you can hold her.'

Pat glanced at the girl, but she had closed her eyes again. She lay passively all the time while Pat washed her and changed the sheets, which the nurse had had the forethought to bring with her.

'It's amazing how many times I have to use me own sheets.' Pat laughed. 'And I've brought you some baby clothes too. I keep a few spares. Now, you have a little sleep whilst I wash the baby and then you can hold her.'

To Pat's dismay the only response Anna made was to turn her face to the wall.

When she had washed and dressed the baby, Pat sighed as she sat in the chair beside the warm fire, holding the child close. She brushed her lips against the tiny infant's downy hair and asked softly, 'What's going to happen to you, little one?'

The firelight was a soft glow on Pat's round face and glinted on her blonde curls, which were usually tucked neatly away beneath her district nurse's severe hat. Her blue eyes were troubled as she looked up and asked quietly, 'What's going on here, Eddie?'

Eddie moved closer to the fire to sit beside Pat. He passed his hand wearily across his forehead. 'I don't know, love, any more than you do. All I can tell you is – ' he glanced across to the bed in the corner, but Anna was now sleeping – 'it looks like she's run away from home. She's desperate that no one should know she's here. She didn't want me to fetch you, even though she was obviously in pain. She's terrified someone is going to find her. Her family, I suppose.'

Pat nodded and sighed. 'Same old story, I expect. She's got pregnant and her family's given her a hard time about it. She's either run away or – ' her tone hardened – 'they've thrown her out.' There was silence between them before Pat added angrily, 'You'd think, wouldn't you, after what we've all been through in the war, that folks would have learnt to be a bit more understanding. It breaks my heart to think of all the poor little bairns born in the war that'll never know their fathers, even some of 'em born *in* wedlock ne'er mind those that weren't. And there's a few of both sorts round here, let me tell you. Ee, what's the world coming to, Eddie? What's the world coming to?'

Eddie was silent, unwilling to admit, even to Pat, that his own wife had shown the same lack of compassion towards Anna.

'But you'd better be careful, Eddie, letting her stay here. She can only be seventeen or eighteen at the most. Legally, still a minor.'

'Well, I'm not going to report her, if that's what you're suggesting.'

'I'm not,' Pat said swiftly, 'but you ought to talk to her when she's stronger. Make her see that she should at least get in touch with her family.'

'She's never mentioned anything about her family, and when I've tried to ask her about herself she clams up.'

Pat glanced across at the bed in the corner. 'Mm. Something's not right, Eddie. Have you seen that scar on her fingers?'

Eddie stared at her and then shook his head.

Pat held up her right hand and with her left fore-finger, made a slashing movement across the first two fingers on her right hand. 'She's got a nasty wound across here. A deep cut, I'd say. It's healed now, but it's not an old scar. I reckon it's been done about six or seven months ago. About the time,' she added point-edly, 'that she would find out she was pregnant.'

There was silence between them, each busy with their own thoughts, until Eddie said, 'I'd better check on the sheep.'

Minutes later, he put his head round the door. 'There's one going into labour and there's not much room in there—'

'Well, you can't bring it in here.'

Eddie shrugged and was about to disappear again when he paused and asked, 'What about you? Do you want me to take you home?'

'No, no. I'll stay here the night.' She cast a coy look at him. 'Though what it'll do to my reputation, I daren't think.'

'Well—' Eddie scratched his head.

Pat laughed. 'Go on with you, you old softy. I'm only teasing. I must stay here till morning anyway and make sure Anna knows how to feed her baby.'

'Oh, right,' Eddie said and looked relieved. He grinned at her before disappearing back into the neighbouring room.

How nice it was, Eddie was thinking as he knelt beside his ewe, to have a woman with a sense of fun and a bit of sparkle about her. Yes, that was the word he would use to describe Pat Jessop. Despite the sadness she had experienced in her own life, there was always a sparkle about her.

It was two o'clock in the morning before Eddie came back into the kitchen, washed himself thoroughly in the sink and sat down wearily in the chair beside the fire. 'The rest seem OK for the moment. What a day!' He leant his head back against the chair and closed his eyes.

'Sorry I couldn't offer to come and help you. It'd've been just like the old days,' Pat said softly. 'How's the lamb?'

'Fine and healthy and suckling straight away.'

'Mm,' Pat said dryly as she glanced towards the sleeping girl in the corner of the room. 'I've always said the animals can teach us a thing or two.' She paused and then said, 'Tell you what, Eddie, you nurse this little mite for a moment and I'll make us some tea and then you get a bit of rest.'

'What about you?' Eddie asked as Pat gently placed the sleeping infant in his arms.

'Me? Oh, I'm all right. Quite used to the odd sleepless night, but you'll have to take me back to the village in the morning. I've me rounds to do. In fact' – she smiled impishly – 'you'd better get me back home before it's light, else there'll be gossip.'

Eddie chuckled softly, but his eyes were now on the baby in his arms. 'She's a bonny little thing, ain't she?'

'She is,' Pat agreed, once again watching the gentle expression on Eddie's face and feeling the prickle of tears behind her eyelids.

In her job, Pat Jessop rarely let her emotions get the better of her. It didn't mean she didn't care. Far from it. Her compassion was what made her so good at her job and loved by all her patients. But the whole village knew that Eddie's marriage was not all that it might have been. And Pat's tender heart went out to the man who had been her friend since childhood.

'Funny woman, that Bertha,' was what the gossips said. 'Her dad was a right 'un. Affairs? He 'ad more women than I've had 'ot dinners. And what he didn't get up to in the war was nobody's business.' Here, the storyteller would tap the side of his nose and nod knowingly. 'Black market. Mind you, if you wanted owt, you knew where to go. There wasn't much that Wilf Tinker couldn't lay his hands on.'

'Where is he now then? Dead?'

'Oh no.' The teller would warm to his tale, saying triumphantly, 'He's inside.'

'Never!'

'S'right, but the family don't want folks to know. As if we don't all know already.'

'What happened?'

'It was near the end of the war. Several of the farmers were having ducks pinched in the night. Course, good source of food, weren't it, on the black market? Well, Wilf's driving his old van one night along a country lane in the middle of nowhere when the local bobby stops him. "I ain't no ducks," Wilf ses straight away and then, of course, the bobby looks in the back of the van and finds half a dozen of the little beggars. Still alive, mind you, in a sort of coop and covered over with sacks to muffle the quacking. Daft part about it was – ' at this point the storyteller would be almost overcome with mirth – 'the bobby'd only stopped Wilf 'cos one of his headlamps was showing a bit too much light. He weren't even looking for ducks.'

All this ran through Pat Jessop's mind as she watched the infant lying in the strong arms of Eddie Appleyard. She felt guilty that she had played a part in his present unhappy marriage. Much as she had adored her husband and never once regretted falling head over heels in love with him and marrying him, she did regret that this had perhaps precipitated Eddie into taking up with Bertha Tinker. If only he hadn't, she reflected, then maybe now . . .

'Here's your tea, Eddie,' she said, placing it on the

floor beside him. 'Let me have her.' She held out her arms once more for the child. 'Drink that and then get your head down for an hour or two. You're going to have a few busy days and nights ahead of you.'

In the early hours, before it was quite light, Pat woke Anna.

'I'll have to go soon, ducky, and I want to make sure you know how to feed the little mite.' Whilst Anna made no effort to resist Pat unfastening her clothes and putting the baby to her breast, she made no attempt to hold the child against her. She refused even to put her arms beneath the baby to support it. The baby girl nuzzled against the reluctantly offered breast but made no attempt to suckle.

'They sometimes take a bit of time to learn how to do it. Come on, love. You must hold her. She can't do it all on her own.'

But the girl lay with her head turned to one side, her eyes closed, and refused even to look down at her child.

Pat sighed but continued to support the child, holding her so that the tiny mouth felt the red nipple. After what seemed a long time to the man watching, the baby began to suck.

'There's a clever girl,' Pat talked soothingly to the child. 'That's wonderful. Sometimes they take a lot of coaxing,' she told the new mother, 'but this little one knows what's good for her. Don't you, my precious?'

Eddie looked on, glancing anxiously from child to mother. It was all right whilst Pat was here, but what was going to happen once she had to leave? Would the girl go on rejecting the child? He knew what to do in the animal world when the mother acted this way, but if it came to dealing with a human being he was lost. He thought about the night Tony had been born. Pat had brought him into the world too and he remembered Bertha's arms reaching eagerly for her son. Whatever else she might be, Eddie could not fault Bertha as a mother. The only sad thing about it was that whatever love Bertha had to give was centred upon the boy and there was none left for her husband.

Pat lifted the baby away from Anna and immediately the infant opened her mouth and began to yell.

'My, my, you're letting us know you like it now you've got the hang of it, aren't you?' Pat laughed and put the baby to her mother's other breast.

Still Anna made no move to look down at her child and Pat and Eddie exchanged a worried glance.

At last the baby's hunger was satisfied and she fell asleep.

'There now, Anna, you can go back to sleep again. You must mind you get plenty of rest. I think she's going to be a very demanding baby. But you're young and strong and you'll cope as long as you're sensible and take care of yourself as well as the child.'

Anna lay with her eyes closed. She made no sign that she had even heard Pat, let alone understood what she was saying.

As the light of dawn filtered into the cottage Pat wrapped the child and laid her in the deep armchair. 'She'll be safe there till you get back, Eddie.' She cast an anxious glance back towards the bed. 'I'm worried about that lass, though,' she said quietly. 'I think I'll ask the doctor to take a look at her. If he can get out here in all this lot.'

Eddie nodded. 'Whatever you think best, Pat. But once I've taken you back, I shan't leave her for long.

I might have to go down to the house . . .' They exchanged a look. 'But I'll come straight back.'

'Fetch me again tonight, Eddie.'

'If you're sure?'

Pat nodded firmly. 'I am. Besides by the look of some of those ewes in there, you could use another pair of hands.'

Eddie returned to the cottage later, bringing the puppy back with him from the stable, just in case Bertha heard its yapping and decided to investigate. As he opened the door, he found the baby crying again, but Anna had made no effort to get up from her bed. She was just lying there with her eyes closed, a tiny frown furrowing her brow as if the noise was irritating her.

At once the puppy trotted across the floor and, taking little runs, tried to jump up onto the bed, barking excitedly. Anna opened her eyes, leant down and lifted it onto the bed. She fondled its silky ears and even smiled gently at it. Eddie watched in disbelief to see that the girl could fuss a dog and yet turn away from her own child. Determinedly, he crossed the room and lifted the puppy from the bed and carried it to its basket in the opposite corner.

'Stay,' he instructed sternly. The little thing whimpered, but lay down obediently, its nose resting on its paws, its eyes large and appealing.

Then Eddie picked up the child and carried her to the bed. 'This is the one you should be taking notice of. You must feed her, love. You're all she's got. Come along now.'

But Anna turned her face towards the wall again and refused to answer.

'Look, lass. I don't want to have to do what the midwife did—' He bit his lip at the thought of having to put the child to the mother's breast himself. He took a deep breath. 'But I will, if you force me to it, 'cos I'm not going to stand by and see her go hungry.'

Suddenly, she turned her head to face him angrily. 'I don't want it,' she cried out passionately above the noise of her child's crying. 'I *hate* it. I don't care if it dies. And me along with it. Just leave us. Let us both die. It'd be for the best.'

Appalled, Eddie stared at her. Then he said firmly, 'This little mite doesn't deserve to be spoken about like that. *She's* done no wrong.' He couldn't prevent the obvious emphasis, but immediately he regretted his words.

Anna raised herself on one elbow. For the first time there was real spirit in her tone. 'What right have you to judge me? You don't know the first thing about me. You don't know what happened.'

'Then tell me.'

'It's none of your business.' She lay back down again. 'I don't know why you're bothering with us, anyway. Just let us be.'

'If I just "let you be" as you put it, you'll let this little one die, won't you? And then you'll be in trouble yourself.'

'No, I won't,' she muttered. ''Cos I won't be here either.'

'Don't talk silly, Anna,' Eddie said. 'Sit up and feed this little one. Come on.' His tone was authoritative now, but still it had no effect. The girl turned her whole body away from him and her child and lay on her side facing the wall.

Eddie sighed and laid the baby back in the big

armchair. There was nothing else for it. He'd have to feed the child himself the way he sometimes fed motherless lambs.

For the rest of the day Eddie tended the baby and his sheep. He warmed milk on the fire and dipped a teaspoon in boiling water to cleanse it. Then, when it was cool enough, he sat with the child on his knee and painstakingly spooned the milk into the baby's mouth.

He kept his eye on Anna, but spoke to her only briefly to give her some food.

'Anything else you want?' he asked abruptly. Anna shook her head, unwilling to meet his gaze.

It wasn't that he was deliberately punishing her, it was just that he didn't know how to deal with her callous treatment of the child. To see her fondle the puppy but turn her back on her baby had made him angry.

Late in the afternoon another ewe gave birth to a healthy lamb. Eddie placed the newborn creature to the mother's teat and at once the lamb began to suck, the mother patiently giving herself to her young.

From her bed, Anna heard the bleating and could picture the scene – the new mother and her offspring. When Eddie came back into the room, Anna had raised herself on one elbow and was looking across the room towards her own child, lying quietly now in the chair.

She glanced briefly at Eddie, but then lay down again and closed her eyes. She was sore and ached all over. And she was tired, so very, very tired. All she wanted to do was lie here and not have to move ever again. For months she had tried to ignore the inevitable. And since Eddie had brought her to this cottage, she had begun to feel that, perhaps, she could begin to live again, that the nightmare would begin to fade. But now, after the birth, she would have a daily reminder. Every time she looked at the child, the memories would come flooding back. Anna was fighting an internal emotional battle that the man could know nothing about, nor even begin to guess at.

Ten

That evening Eddie again fetched Pat Jessop from the village on his tractor.

'I hope, for your sake, nobody sees us,' Pat said.

Eddie shrugged. 'They'll just think I'm taking you to some outlying place 'cos of the weather.'

'Which you are,' she smiled. 'Just as long as they don't guess exactly *where* it is you're taking me. Anyway, how is she?'

Pat's face became anxious as Eddie explained what he had been obliged to do to feed the child. 'She doesn't want owt to do with the bairn, Pat. I'm worried sick.'

Pat put her hand briefly on his arm. 'Don't worry, Eddie. If the worst comes to the worst, I'll bring the child back here and look after it myself. I've a good neighbour who'd look after her whilst I'm out on my rounds. She's seven of her own.' Pat laughed. 'She'd hardly notice another one to feed. Jessie'd take it all in her stride.'

Eddie smiled briefly, but said, 'Well, I hope it won't have to come to that.'

'I hope so too. Come on, we'd better get back there and see what this night brings.'

To their disappointment, it brought no change in Anna's attitude. True, Pat was able to make her feed the child, but she could not coax Anna to hold the baby nor even to look at it properly.

87

In the early morning Pat found herself in the neighbouring room, delivering a lamb whilst Eddie attended to another ewe.

In the cosiness of the cottage, cut off from the rest of the world by the swirling snow outside, Eddie and Pat smiled at each other. 'It's just like when I used to come and help you and your dad when we were little, Eddie.'

Eddie's dark eyes held her gaze in the flickering light from the hurricane lamp. Her lovely face glowed in the soft light and her gentle eyes held such compassion, such understanding and, yes, love. He was sure he could see love in her eyes. 'Aye,' he said softly. 'I remember.' He sighed and murmured, 'Oh Pat, if only—'

She touched his arm. 'Don't, Eddie,' she whispered, a catch in her voice. 'Please don't say it.'

They gazed at each other for a long moment, each knowing instinctively what the other was thinking, before Pat stood up and deliberately broke the spell.

But it was a moment between them that she would cherish.

When Eddie and Pat left just before dawn, the cottage was quiet. Slowly, Anna sat up and looked across to where her daughter lay. The child was quiet now, full of her milk, which, the midwife had told her, was going to be plentiful.

'You must drink plenty of milk yourself and eat well,' Pat had urged her and had left a bowl of cereal and a glass of milk beside the bed. 'And please, ducky, try to feed the bairn yourself.'

'It – hurts,' the girl had said. She had touched her own breasts. 'They're hard.'

'It's the milk coming.' Deviously, and keeping her tone deliberately casual, Pat had added, 'It would help that feeling if you fed her.'

But, yet again, Anna had turned away. Now, in the stillness of early morning, she lay back and drifted into sleep again but was awakened by the door opening very quietly. For once, she could not even summon up the terror that usually assailed her. She just lay there keeping her eyes closed. Whoever it was, she had not the strength to do anything about it. Just as before, she had not had the strength . . .

She winced, screwing up her eyes tightly to block out the terrifying memories.

Tony tiptoed across the floor, pausing to look down at the baby lying fast asleep in the chair. Then he came to stand by the bed.

'Are you all right?' he whispered, afraid to wake her if she was sleeping.

Anna nodded, but did not speak. She did not even open her eyes.

'Where's me dad?'

Again, there was no answer.

He tried again. 'Is it a boy or a girl?'

Silence. A little more loudly he repeated his question.

Anna licked her dry, cracked lips. 'A girl.'

'What are you going to call her?'

Anna let out a long, deep sigh that seemed to come from the very depths of her being. 'I don't know,' she said dully.

'You'll have to call her something,' the boy said practically and wrinkled his brow thoughtfully, as if the whole burden of naming the child rested with him. Perhaps it did, for the mother was uninterested. 'What about Alice?' he ventured. At school, the teacher had just been reading *Alice's Adventures in Wonderland* to the class. It was the first name that came to his mind.

There was no response from Anna. 'There's Rose or Janet or Mary . . .' He ticked the suggestions off on his fingers, naming the girls in his class. At last, as if wearying of his persistence, Anna opened her eyes and said, 'Maisie. Her name's Maisie.'

'Maisie,' the boy repeated, sounding the name out aloud. 'Maisie Woods. Yes, it sounds nice. I like it.'

The child began to whimper and Tony grinned. 'See, she knows her name already.'

Very gently, he picked up the child and carried her to the bed. 'She wants her mummy, don't you, Maisie?'

He tried to lay the child in Anna's arms, but she made no move to take her. 'Come on,' he said a little impatiently. 'She's hungry. She wants feeding.'

Anna stared down at the child. The baby's crying ceased for a moment. Dark blue eyes stared at her mother. Whether or not the tiny infant could really see her, Anna did not know, but it seemed as if she could. The baby's face worked, stretching and grimacing.

'Look, she's smiling at you,' Tony said, his knowledge of human babies too sketchy to think otherwise.

Slowly, tentatively, Anna slipped her left arm beneath the baby's head. With her right hand she gently pulled down the shawl and looked upon her daughter for the first time.

When Eddie returned to the cottage, Anna was feeding her daughter and Tony, without a shred of embarrassment, was sitting on the end of the bed watching her.

To the young boy, it was perfectly natural to see a mother feeding her young.

Eddie felt relief flood through him. Only later would he learn that it had been his son's prompting that had finally broken down Anna's defences.

He came towards the bed, smiling. 'All right, lass?' Anna looked up, managed a weak smile and nodded.

'I've brought a few things to stock up your pantry.' He glanced at Tony. 'You'd better get back home, lad. Your mam knows I'm going to be up here for the next few days. With the sheep,' he added pointedly.

The boy stared at him for a moment, then looked away. He understood his father's unspoken insinuation. 'Can I – can I come up each day? I shan't be going to school 'cos of the roads, but I can get up here, specially now your tractor's made some tracks.'

'Only if your mam ses you can.'

The boy nodded eagerly. 'She'll want to send you some food anyway.'

Eddie put his hand on Tony's shoulder. 'Now, you look after your mam. Let me know straight away if she needs owt. All right?'

The boy nodded, grinned at Anna and then reached out and gently touched the baby's head. ''Bye, Maisie,' he whispered softly.

As he left, Eddie asked, 'Is that her name? Maisie?'

Anna's voice was husky. 'Yes. Tony – wanted me to decide on a name.'

Quietly, Eddie said, 'It doesn't matter yet, but you do know you'll have to register her birth, don't you? It's the law.'

Anna looked at him with startled eyes. 'How – how would I have to do that?'

91

'Go into town and—'

'Oh, I couldn't.'

'But you must register her.'

Her eyes were wide with fear. 'I couldn't go into town.'

Eddie sighed and let the matter drop for the moment. Perhaps he could get Pat to deal with the problem.

Pat beamed with delight when she entered the cottage that evening to find Anna sitting up in the bed, cuddling the child to her breast. She stamped the snow from her boots and shook her coat.

'It's snowing again,' Pat remarked as she crossed the room towards Anna. Making no direct comment about the change in the girl, she merely enquired, 'All right, ducky?'

Anna nodded. 'Thank you,' she said huskily, 'for all you've done.'

Pat shrugged. 'It's me job, love.' But the look in Anna's dark eyes told the midwife that she understood Pat Jessop had done far more for her than was usual.

'Now then,' Pat said briskly, 'we'll banish Eddie to the other room while I help you have a good wash. I've brought you some clean sheets and a nightie. And there's some clothes for the bairn. Now, off you go, Eddie, and see to your sheep.' Pat smiled at him and flapped her hand to dismiss him.

Eddie grinned as he closed the door behind him, marvelling at how Pat Jessop got her own way without even raising her voice. With her merry face and good-humoured banter, people just did as she asked them without arguing. He shook his head thoughtfully, unable to prevent himself once more comparing Pat's methods to his wife's sharp, demanding ways.

With a minimum of fuss, Anna was soon washed and lying in a clean flannelette nightdress between crisp, sweet-smelling sheets. Then Pat turned her attention to the baby. For a while, Anna lay watching her bathing the child in a tin bath that Eddie had brought from his barn, murmuring endearments to the wriggling infant all the while.

'You're a lovely little thing, aren't you, my precious. With those big eyes and such a lot of pretty hair.' Pat glanced up at Anna and smiled. 'I think she's going to be a real carrot top, love. Just look at her pretty hair.'

Anna's eyes widened and her lips parted in a gasp. With a noise that sounding suspiciously like a cry of despair, Anna turned her back on them both and buried her head in her pillow.

Pat watched her, biting her lip and frowning worriedly. *Now what have I said?* she thought.

She laid the child down in the deep armchair and went towards the bed. Touching the girl's shaking shoulder, she said softly, 'I'm sorry, love. I didn't mean to upset you. Would you like to tell me about it?'

The girl's only reply was to shake her head.

Pat sighed. In all her years of experience, she had never come across a case like this before. She'd dealt with mothers who had rejected their children initially, but once they came around, as she had believed Anna had done, then they didn't often lapse back into withdrawing themselves from their child. Yet now, it seemed, she had unwittingly touched some raw nerve that had made this girl turn her back on her child once more.

She patted the girl's shoulder again, feeling power-less. It was a feeling she did not often experience and certainly did not relish. She liked to be able to help people and, most of the time, she did. 'I'm a good listener, love. And I never judge folk. Whatever it is that's upsetting you, it'll not be anything I've not heard before. So, if you ever want a kindly ear, you know where I am. Your secret – whatever it is – would be safe with me.'

The girl's shoulder was rigid beneath Pat's touch and she made no movement, gave no sign that she had even heard the nurse's words.

Later, when Anna had fallen into a restless sleep and the baby was quiet, Eddie and Pat sat before the fire.

'I said summat to upset her, Eddie,' Pat whispered. 'Just as she seemed to be coming round an' all. I could kick mesen.'

'What did you say?'

Pat sighed and shook her head. 'I was just talking to her about how pretty the child is. With big, dark eyes and that she's going to be a redhead.'

They sat in silence for a moment before Eddie said thoughtfully, 'Perhaps it reminds her of someone. Some-one she'd rather forget?'

Pat stared at him. 'Oh. The – the father, you mean?'

Soberly, Eddie nodded. He opened his mouth to say more, but at that moment there was scuffling outside the back door.

With a worried expression, Eddie got up, 'This can't be Tony. Not at this time of night. Surely—'

As he moved across the room, the door was flung open and a rotund figure, wrapped in thick clothes and covered in snow, stepped into the kitchen. Behind her came a much smaller figure, a figure that scurried into the room and flung itself against Eddie.

'I tried to stop her coming, Dad. Really I did,' Tony cried, tears running down his cold face and mingling with the snow.

Eddie put his arm about the boy, 'It's all right, son. It's all right,' he said gently, as he looked up to face his wife.

Eleven

Bertha's glance took in the girl in the bed, now awakened and sitting up, her eyes fearful. The commotion woke the baby, who began to wail, and Bertha's face contorted into a look of loathing. She swung round and, with surprising agility, flew at her husband, her arms flailing, her hands reaching to slap and punch and scratch. He tried to defend himself as her blows rained upon him, whilst Tony pulled at her coat, crying, 'Mam, Mam, don't. Please, don't.'

Pat hurried forward to intervene, but Bertha shrieked, 'You keep out of this, Pat Jessop. I might 'ave known you'd be in on this.' Then she raised her hand and dealt her husband a stinging blow on his cheek that sent him reeling. Before he had time to recover his senses, Bertha had whirled about and was moving to where the child lay, her hands outstretched, her eyes murderous.

Pat moved, but there was someone even quicker than she was. Anna flung back the bedclothes and seemed to fly across the room. She snatched up her child and hugged her close. 'Don't you touch her. Don't you dare lay a finger on her.'

Her eyes blazing, she faced the irate woman and even Bertha faltered in the face of the lioness protecting her young.

'Bertha, please—' Pat began, but Bertha now turned and vented her anger on the midwife.

'I told you, keep out of this. You've done enough. I suppose you know all about his goings on, do you? And if you know, then the whole village'll know. Aye, an' half Ludthorpe too, I shouldn't wonder.'

'You've no cause to talk to me like that, Bertha.' Pat bristled. 'And you're not being fair to Eddie—'

'Oho, "Eddie", is it? Summat going on between the two of you, is there?' Her face twisted into an ugly sneer. 'Now the war's over you'll have to look a bit nearer home for fellers, won't you?'

Pat was furious. 'How dare you—?'

'Oh, I dare all right. It was common gossip about you cycling up to that RAF camp *and* afore your husband was killed, an' all.' Her mouth twisted and she flung her arm out towards Anna. 'You're no better than that trollop there, Pat Jessop, so don't try to play the innocent with me.'

Pat was shaking her head sadly now. 'You're not right in the head, Bertha. Do you know that? You're twisted, saying such things. I'm a district nurse, for heaven's sake and the camp was in my district.'

Bertha's mouth curled with disbelief. 'Expect me to believe that? They'd got their own doctors and nurses. So why would they need your—' she paused deliberately – 'services?'

'Oh, there's no reasoning with you, Bertha. I was often called to the families of RAF personnel who lived near the camp. And I'll tell you something, whether you want to hear it or not. I don't care what you say about me, but you've no call to make such horrible insinuations about Eddie.' Pat shook her forefinger in Bertha's face. 'You've got a good man there, and you're a fool not to see it.'

'How would you know?'

'Come off it, Bertha. I've known Eddie all me life. Do you really expect me to call him "Mr Appleyard" now? 'Cos if you do, then you've another think coming.'

All the time the heated exchange was taking place between the two women, Tony had clung to his father. Anna clutched her baby to her, patting the child's back and trying to soothe her crying.

'If you're so clever, then, Nurse Jessop, p'raps you'd like to tell me what's really going on then with this girl here?'

'Like he told you, Bertha. She was in the marketplace in town with nowhere to go and he took pity on her. That's all.'

Bertha snorted. 'If you believe that, then it's you that's the fool. Not me.'

She turned and held out her hand to her son. 'Come on, Tony. You an' me's going home. You're not to come up here again. You hear me?'

Tony cast a helpless glance at his father. 'But – but we haven't told him why we came.' He glanced nervously at his mother, yet he was determined to speak out. 'It's the sheep in the barn. There's one or two of them dropping their lambs. And one – well – you ought to come, Dad.' His voice petered away as his mother added, 'Oh, he's far more important things to do up here, Tony love. I see that now. And I also see why you tried to stop me coming.'

The boy hung his head and shrank against his father, but Bertha was holding out her fat arms towards her son. 'But I don't blame you, lovey. It's not your fault. You're not old enough to understand. Come on, love. Come to your mammy.'

Eddie gripped the boy's shoulder understandingly

and then gave him a gentle push. 'Go on, son,' he said quietly.

'But what about the sheep, Dad?'

Eddie nodded. 'I'll come down.'

With obvious reluctance, the boy moved towards his mother. She put her arm about his shoulders and drew him to her. Her eyes narrowed as she said, 'You and your carryings on, Eddie, are one thing, but involving your own son in your lies and deceit is quite another. I'll never forgive you for that. Never.'

And then she was gone, out into the wild night, dragging the boy with her and leaving the three adults staring after her, mesmerized and beginning to wonder if it had all really happened.

'I'm so sorry,' Anna began. 'It's all my fault. I should never have let you bring me with you that night. I'll go.'

Eddie spread his hands in a helpless gesture. 'You can't go anywhere in this lot, love.' He sighed heavily as he sank into the armchair, weary and dispirited. He dropped his head into his hands as he muttered. 'Wait till the weather improves and you're feeling stronger, then we'll see.'

The truth was that, deep inside him, he didn't want her to go anywhere. Eddie wanted Anna to stay right here in his little cottage.

Pat seemed to recover her senses. 'Get back into bed, love. Here, give me the bairn. There, there,' she crooned as she took the crying child into her arms. 'All that shouting's upset you, hasn't it, my little love? There, there. It's all over and your mammy's going to feed you now.'

Anna climbed back into the bed and soon a comparative peace was restored as the infant's cries were silenced while she sucked hungrily. But the cosy, intimate atmosphere of the little cottage was gone, spoiled by Bertha's bitter wrath.

When mother and child were sleeping, Eddie and Pat sat before the fire, their heads close together.

'What are you going to do, Eddie?'

Eddie closed his eyes and sighed wearily. Then, as the baby stirred and gave a little snuffling sound in her sleep, he smiled. He seemed to straighten up as he glanced towards Anna lying in the bed. 'D'you know,' he said, as if he was as surprised as Pat to hear himself saying the words, 'I reckon I'm going to stand up to Bertha for once in me life.'

Pat touched his hand. 'Good for you.'

'The lass and her bairn can stay as long as they want. If – if she wants to go – ' Pat saw a fleeting expression of disappointment in his eyes – 'then – so be it. But if she wants to stay, then she can.' He stood up and pulled on his coat. 'I'd best be off and see to me sheep.' He paused at the door and turned to say solemnly, 'There's one thing Bertha was right about, though.'

Pat raised her eyebrows. She couldn't think of a single thing that the vitriolic woman had been right about.

Eddie went on, 'Tony. I shouldn't have involved him. I'll have to tell him not to come here any more.'

Pat smiled as she said softly, 'You can try, but I don't think either you – or Bertha – will be able to stop him.'

The snow ceased at last, but then came the thaw and, with it, the danger of flooding to the surrounding district.

'You can't stay here. You'll have to go into the village,' Eddie told Anna. 'Pat's said she'll have you and the bairn. I'll take you—'

'No!' Anna's voice was sharp and determined. She was up and about now and able to care for herself and her child and even the puppy, but she was not yet fully recovered from the birth and had not ventured outside the cottage except to visit the privy. 'We're going nowhere. Not yet, anyway. Not until I'm well enough to move on. To get right away.'

Eddie spread his hands. 'But this cottage lies almost at the lowest point in the vale. The stream will overflow. There's no doubt about that happening, and when it does the water could back up as far as here. It'll get into the cottage—'

'Then we'll go upstairs.'

'You can't do that. The whole place would be damp. You wouldn't be able to keep the bairn warm. You can't light a fire up there.'

'Can't you bring me a paraffin heater, or something?'

'I could,' Eddie agreed reluctantly, 'but it would hardly keep you warm enough up there.'

'We'll be fine.'

'You might be, but what about the baby?' He eyed her thoughtfully. She seemed to have come round now and to be caring for her child properly. Pat had no worries, but Eddie couldn't stop the dreadful suspicion that the girl was just biding her time and that perhaps she still hoped something would happen to the child. To both of them, if it came to that. He lay awake at night, alone now in the spare bedroom to which Bertha had banished him, thinking of the young girl in the cottage and wondering . . .

'Maisie'll be fine,' Anna was insisting now. 'I'll keep

her warm.' She must have seen the anxiety in his face, for she added, in her soft, husky voice, 'I promise.'

As the snow melted and the earth began to show through in brown patches, it was still too wet for the sheep to find grazing, even though they were out on the hillside again. Each day Eddie brought hay for his sheep, but each night Anna still found them huddled against the cottage wall, as if asking to be let in. And each night she would open the door wide and usher them into the room, comforted by the sound of their soft bleating in the middle of the night.

'The stream's overflowing like I said it would. I've brought you some sandbags, but I don't reckon it'll hold the water from getting into the cottage.'

Anna nodded. 'I saw. I went out for the first time today. I took Buster for a walk.' She laughed. 'But he doesn't like getting his paws wet.'

Eddie smiled, though the worry never quite left his eyes. 'He's only little.'

'I've got everything ready in the room upstairs.'

'I'm sorry now that I didn't get Joe Wainwright up here to the roof afore Christmas.'

Anna shrugged and smiled. 'One room's all right. That's all we need.' She glanced at him, teasing. 'I wasn't thinking of taking the sheep up there an' all.'

Eddie laughed. 'No, I don't think they'd manage to climb the ladder. Not even with Rip barking at their heels.' He watched her for a moment. It was the first time that Anna had said something light-hearted and now he saw that she looked better – calmer, he thought, and not so afraid.

'Are you happy here?' he asked before he stopped to

think. To his chagrin, the smile faded from her face and the haunted look was at once back in her eyes. She returned his gaze, but avoided answering his question directly.

'I'm very grateful for what you've done for me, Eddie.' Suddenly, she was on her guard again as she added, 'I'll – I'll always be grateful to you, but I can't stay here for ever.'

'Why? Why not, love? You said you'd nowhere to go.' He paused, then when she did not answer he pressed on. 'Or is it different now you've had the bairn? Is that it? Are you going home—?'

Almost before the words were out of his mouth, she had spat back. 'No, no. Never.' Then she faltered. 'I – I have no home.'

'All right, lass, all right.' He spread his hands, trying to placate her. 'I didn't mean to upset you and I'm not trying to pry. It's just that – ' he took a deep breath – 'it's just that I'd miss you if you did go and – and – well—' He was floundering now and the words came out in a rush. 'If you really haven't anywhere special to go, you're welcome to stay here.'

'What about your wife?' Her unusual dark eyes were regarding him steadily.

He shrugged. 'She's said no more about it. The only thing she has done is to stop Tony from coming to see you.' He forbore to tell Anna that his wife had also banished him from her bed. Not that it was any great loss. She had not allowed any 'marital relations', as they called it, for years, he thought bitterly. The only thing he did miss was the warmth of her bulk next to him on a cold night. But a brick heated in the oven, wrapped in a piece of blanket and shoved into the bed was a good substitute! Now he smiled mischievously.

103

'But I don't expect for one minute that she'll be able to stop him sneaking over the hill to see you now and again. That lad will find a way, if I'm not much mistaken.'

Anna's small smile chased away some of the guarded look on her face. 'Well,' she said slowly, 'I'd like to stay for a while longer, but I don't want to cause you any more trouble.'

'You won't,' he said briefly and silently added to himself: *No more than I'd already got afore you came.*

Twelve

The snow continued to melt and the rushing stream became a torrent, which overflowed its banks and flooded the land. Nearer and nearer it crept to the cottage and Anna was obliged to move upstairs, though she could wade through the water if she needed to in her wellingtons. Eddie helped her take her bedding up the narrow ladder and lift the armchair onto the table, so that it would not get soaked.

'I still wish you'd go and stay with Pat Jessop. She asked about you again yesterday.'

'That was kind of her,' Anna said carefully. 'But we'll be fine up there, specially now you've brought us that little stove. As long as I can keep Maisie safe and warm and fed, we'll be all right.'

'But can you?' Eddie asked worriedly.

Anna regarded him steadily. 'If I can't, Eddie, I promise you I'll give in and let you take us to Nurse Jessop's.'

'That's all right then, lass.' He smiled with relief. 'And now I'd better get these sheep onto higher ground.'

'How's the lambing going?' Anna asked. 'I wish I could be more help to you.'

'Considering what we've had to cope with, very well, really. I've still several ewes to drop, but I've already got a good few healthy lambs.' He raised his hand. 'Must get on, lass. See you later.'

''Bye,' Anna murmured as she watched him whistle to Rip and begin to round up the sheep that had been her companions for several days. She was sorry to see them go.

The water was now lapping at the walls of the cottage and against the sandbags across the thresholds. As Anna sat on the floor at the top of the ladder with the puppy beside her, the water began to seep into her home. Buster yapped excitedly, as if he could drive back the thing invading the cottage. They watched tiny rivulets creep beneath the door and spread out, until the whole of the earth floor was covered. And still the water kept coming.

She felt a moment's panic, imagining it rising so high that it engulfed the whole cottage and drowned them.

And suddenly she wanted to live. She no longer felt the craving to lie down and let a welcome oblivion overtake her. Now she had something, or rather someone, to live for. She had another human being dependent upon her. She hadn't wanted the child. It had grown within her against her will and she had hated it. Hated the thing inside because of how it had come to be there.

But now the child was no longer an 'it'. Maisie was a tiny human being in her own right, already with a character that was evident when she bellowed for attention. Anna smiled fondly as she glanced over her shoulder to where her child lay sleeping in a Moses basket that Pat Jessop had brought. Where had she heard the phrase 'They bring their love with them'? Well, it was certainly true of her Maisie. Now Anna loved her daughter with a fierce, protective passion. And, ironically, it had been Bertha Appleyard who had made her see that.

If only – Anna's face clouded – the child had not been born with red hair.

She glanced down again at the water, still rising below her. Rationally, she worked out that, because of the lie of the land, the water could not possibly rise above a certain depth. Up here, they would be quite safe.

That night Anna lay down on the soft featherbed mattress on the floor and cuddled her child to her.

Though the water lapped beneath them, she felt safer than she had done for weeks. Cut off from the outside world by the flooding, no one could find her.

'Still visiting ya little bastard, are ya?'

Eddie sighed deeply and cast a sideways glance at Tony sitting at the table, head bowed and toying with the food on his plate.

'Bertha, the child's not mine. How many more times—?'

Bertha snorted. 'She's got brown hair. Just like you. I saw that much that night.'

Holding onto his patience with a supreme effort, Eddie said, 'No, she hasn't. It's red. Ginger. And her eyes are blue.'

'That's nowt to go by. All newborn babies have blue eyes.' She nodded knowingly. 'Its eyes'll be brown and its hair'll go darker. Like yours.'

Bertha pursed her small mouth until it almost disappeared into her fat face. She banged Eddie's dinner onto the table in front of him and then took her place opposite, beside Tony.

'Don't you worry, love.' She patted her son's arm. 'You've still got me, even if your dad is so taken up with his new daughter that he hasn't any time for you now.'

'That's not true, Bertha—'

Bertha's tone was vitriolic. 'Isn't it? You're off up that track two or three times a day and you don't come back for an hour or more. And don't try telling me you're with your sheep all that time, 'cos most of 'em are down here in the barn or the yard. I bet you're off up there to watch her feeding her kid. Getting an eyeful, are ya? Disgusting, that's what you are.' Her mouth twisted. 'Disgusting.'

Tony's head hung lower as he felt the colour creep up his own face. He'd watched Anna feeding little Maisie. He'd not thought it wrong. So was he 'disgusting' as well, then, in his mother's eyes?

He'd not go to the cottage again, he vowed silently. He didn't want to upset his mam – didn't want her to think that about him. And he didn't want to see the baby any more. Not if his dad was going to love her more than him. Yet he liked going to see Anna and the puppy, and the baby, too, if he was truthful. He'd helped name the little girl. He'd begun to feel she belonged to him a little bit as well. But his mam was so angry. Angry at his dad, angry because the girl was even there. It seemed to him that she hated Anna and the little baby. But he still couldn't understand what his mam meant when she said the baby was his dad's.

The young boy, with a tumult of emotions going on

inside his head that he couldn't really understand or rationalize, pushed the food around his plate and chewed each mouthful round and round, unable to swallow for the lump in his throat.

'You all right, lass?' It was Eddie's voice shouting through the front door.

Anna climbed down the ladder and stepped into the water. She pulled open the door and smiled a welcome. As Eddie stepped inside, she said, 'We're fine. Managing to keep warm and dry.'

'Pat wants to come and see you. Check on you and the bairn, but—'

'Tell her not to worry till this lot's gone. We're all right. Honestly.'

Eddie nodded, but the worried look never left his eyes.

'There's something else, isn't there?' Anna said.

Eddie smiled ruefully. 'I don't think Tony'll be coming to see you any more. His – his mam's put a stop to it.'

'Well, I expected that. I'm sorry, though. I'll miss him.'

'Aye, an' I reckon he'll miss you. He keeps asking about you and Maisie, but—' His voice trailed away.

'But what?' Anna prompted.

Eddie sighed. 'Oh, nothing really.' He didn't want to tell Anna about the full extent of Bertha's spite, though he knew she would guess most of it.

Her presence in the cottage was causing Eddie Appleyard all sorts of problems that he had not foreseen when he had brought the girl home that night. He hadn't known what he was doing, he thought wryly, in more ways than one!

But, despite it all, not for one moment did he regret that Anna had come into his life.

Thirteen

It was late the following afternoon when Anna heard movement outside the cottage and then someone hammering on the front door at the bottom of the ladder. She climbed down and stood near the door, but did not open it.

'Who is it?' she called.

'Me,' came Tony's voice. She pulled open the door, rippling the water further into the cottage.

The boy was breathless from wading through the flood to reach her.

'What are you doing here? You shouldn't—'

'Me dad sent me,' he interrupted. 'He ses can you come down to the farm? He needs help and he ses I'm not big enough to do it.' For a moment, the boy's mouth was a disgruntled pout and there was resentment in his eyes as he looked at her, as if she was personally to blame for taking the place he believed was rightfully his. 'He's got two ewes dropping at once and they're both difficult. He needs help and I can't get to the village—'

'Of course I'll come, but I'll just have to get Maisie wrapped up warm—'

'Dad said not to take her.' His head drooped sulkily. 'I – I'm to stay with her, he said.'

Anna bit her lip, uncertain whether to trust the boy in his present mood, though she really had no choice.

111

Eddie Appleyard had been good to her. In fact, he had probably saved her life and that of her child. She couldn't refuse his plea for help.

'All right then. She's just been fed, so she'll be all right for some time and she's asleep. But don't touch the stove, will you?'

'Course I won't,' he said, vexed that she could doubt his common sense.

She followed him up the ladder and dressed herself quickly in the warmest clothing she had, then, with a last glance at her child, she descended the ladder again and left the cottage. Once out of the water, she hurried up the track towards the farm. She was gratified to find that she had almost recovered from the birth of her child. She was not quite as strong as normal, but youth had helped her to heal quickly.

She paused at the top of the hill to look down at the farm below her. In the low-lying parts of the land, water stood in small lakes, and as she set off down the track she could see that part of Eddie's yard too was under water. As she waded through it to reach the barn, she glanced apprehensively towards the farmhouse, hoping that Bertha would not catch sight of her.

She reached the huge barn door, pulled it open and stepped inside. There were two makeshift pens at one end with straw bales where Eddie could attend to the ewes in labour. Anna pushed her way through the flock, patting a head here, stroking a woolly back there until she reached him.

'I've got a bad one here,' Eddie said. 'Breech and I reckon it's twins.' Then he nodded towards the ewe in the next pen. 'I want you to have a go at that one. The forelegs are presented but there's no sign of the head. Do you know what to do?'

Anna nodded. 'I think so. Push it back very gently and try to manipulate the head into line with the forelegs?'

Eddie gave a quick smile. 'That's it. Your hands are smaller than mine. Tony tried, but his wrist wasn't quite strong enough.'

As she squatted down beside the ewe, Anna smiled ruefully. 'He's not very happy at me taking his place.'

'I'll talk to him later. At the moment I've more to think about than Tony having a mardy.'

There was silence between Eddie and Anna as they struggled to help the ewes. The only noise the bleating from thirty or so sheep.

'There!' Anna said triumphantly, as the lamb slithered safely from its mother. Swiftly she cleaned its mouth. 'It's not breathing, Eddie.' But without waiting for instruction, Anna bent her head close to the tiny creature and blew into its mouth. After a few attempts she looked up, smiling. 'It's fine now.'

'Well done, lass. Mind you dry it well and don't forget to see to the navel.'

'How are you doing?'

'Not good. I think I could lose this ewe. She's quite old and, like I thought, it was twins. I've got them both and they're OK, but she's not cleansing properly.' He shook his head sadly and ruffled the sheep's coat. 'Poor old lass. You've given me a lot of healthy lambs, though, in your time, haven't you?'

'Mine's all right. She's cleansed and I've checked her udders. Do you think she'd take one of those lambs?'

Eddie looked doubtful. 'I'd sooner rear these by the bottle and let her feed her own. One strong lamb's much better than two weaker ones. Mind you,' he said, scratching his head thoughtfully, 'I don't know how I'm going to cope. I've two lambs in the house already and Bertha won't have owt to do with them. Tony's been looking after them, but now the snow's gone he'll have to go back to school. The lane to Wintersby village isn't too bad with flood water.'

'I could take them home with me,' Anna offered.

In the warm cosiness of the barn, they looked at each other. In the soft glow of the lamplight, Eddie marvelled at the girl's beauty. Her eyes were dark pools and in the light from the lamp her skin was a golden colour. And, it was not lost on either of them that she had referred to the tumbledown cottage as 'home'. Tremulously, Anna smiled. 'I've nothing else to do – apart from looking after Maisie – and I could manage to carry them up the ladder.'

'Well, if you're sure, it would help if you could take at least one. I'll bring you bottles and everything you'll need for feeding.'

He glanced at the ewe near Anna. 'Tell you what,' he said, suddenly coming to a decision, 'Let's risk it. She's young and healthy. Let's try her with one of 'em and then you can feed the other. If we can get hers and one of these twins to suckle, we might trick her into thinking she's had the pair of them.'

Eddie picked up one of the lambs and passed it over to Anna, who rubbed some of the adoptive mother's afterbirth fluids over the orphan. She gave it to the ewe to lick first and kept the animal's own offspring back from her until she had accepted the other lamb.

'That's it,' Eddie murmured, not needing to give advice and amazed, yet again, at the young girl's knowledge. *She's been brought up on a farm*, he thought briefly. *She must have been. And she's been taught well.*

It wasn't until late at night that both lambs were

suckling contentedly. Anna stood up and eased her aching limbs. She glanced towards the other pen, an unspoken question on her face. Eddie shook his head. 'Gone, I'm afraid,' he said of the ewe and sighed.

'I'm sorry,' she said. Then she glanced around the barn. 'If there's nothing else I can do, Eddie, I'll be getting back. Maisie must be hungry by now and—'

'Another minute won't hurt, love. Here, sit down and have a drink first. There's a flask of tea I brought out somewhere. Ah, here it is. I reckon we've earned this.'

They sat side by side, leaning against a bale of straw, and sipped the warm, sweet tea gratefully.

'What a night,' Eddie murmured. 'I couldn't have managed without you, lass.'

'We've still lost a ewe, though,' she said sadly.

'Aye, but I'd likely have lost more if you hadn't been here.' He bit his lip, wanting to ask her about her past, wanting to ask how she knew so much about sheep, but he held back the words, knowing that if he so much as mentioned the subject, she would withdraw into silence.

Anna was sitting watching the newborn lambs, a gentle smile on her face. 'Isn't it wonderful—?' she was beginning when the big door of the barn opened and they looked up to see Bertha standing there.

'Eddie? Where are you? Oh, there you are. What do you mean by keeping Tony up all night?' At that moment, she became aware that it was not Tony sitting beside Eddie, but the girl. 'You! What the hell are you doing here?' She glanced around the barn. 'And where's Tony?'

Eddie sighed and struggled to his feet. Wearied by the night's events, the last thing he needed was a confrontation with Bertha. But there was no way out this time. Flatly, he said, 'We've had two difficult births and Tony couldn't help so I sent him to fetch Anna.'

'Oh aye,' Bertha said sarcastically. 'Any excuse.'

'It's not an excuse, Bertha. It's the truth. She's saved me a lamb and possibly a ewe as well, to say nothing of getting this ewe to adopt—'

'Never mind all that. Where's Tony?'

'Looking after Maisie.'

'Maisie?' Bertha glanced around the sheep. 'Which one's Maisie?'

Eddie almost laughed aloud, but the thought of what was going to come in the next few seconds killed his laughter. 'Maisie is Anna's baby.'

For a brief moment Bertha stared at him in disbelief. 'You – you've sent him up there to look after this trollop's bastard?'

'Bertha—' Eddie began, but his wife was in full flow. 'Well, that takes the biscuit, that does. I've heard it all now. I must be the laughing stock of the village. You and your carryings on. For two pins I'd pack me bags and go.' She wagged her forefinger at Eddie. 'And take Tony with me. But I'm not going to, 'cos that's just what you'd like me to do, isn't it? And then you could set up home with your fancy piece here. Well, you aren't going to get what you want, 'cos I'm staying put. I'm not going to see my son done out of his rightful inheritance. Oh no!'

'Bertha, you've got it all wrong.'

'Oh, I don't think so. I'm not blind. But you've a nerve, Eddie Appleyard. Parading your love child for all the world to see as if you're proud—'

'The child isn't his,' Anna said huskily. 'What he's

told you is true. He'd never met me before that night he brought me here. Why won't you believe him?'

Bertha stepped closer and thrust her face close to Anna's. ''Cos I know men. Dirty buggers. Only after one thing.' She prodded a vicious finger into Anna's stomach. '*You* ought to know that.'

Even in the half-light, Eddie could see that Anna's face had turned white.

'That's enough, Bertha. There's no call to say such things to Anna.'

'I've every right. She's no better than a whore and a marriage-wrecker and, mark my words, if the old customs still survived, I'd have her ran-tan-tanned out of here. Yes, that's what I'd do, I'd get the whole village up against her.'

'I'll go,' Anna murmured and picked up the lamb.

'Yes, you go. Get out of my sight and off my boy's land. The quicker you and your bastard leave the better.'

'You'd best go on home,' Eddie said in a low voice. 'I'll bring all the paraphernalia you'll need for feeding.'

As Anna moved away towards the barn door, she could feel the woman's malevolent gaze following her like a knife in her back. And as she hurried across the yard and up the track, her heart was pounding. *We'll go*, she promised herself. *As soon as the flood waters have gone and the weather improves, we'll go.*

It wasn't until she reached the cottage that she began to breathe easily again.

Tony was peering down from the upstairs. 'What happened?' he asked eagerly. 'Is everything all right?'

Huskily, Anna told him, 'I'm afraid we lost a ewe, but she gave us two healthy lambs. Here.' She began to climb the ladder, holding up the lamb. 'Take this one. We managed to get the other ewe, which only had one lamb, to take one of the orphans and I'm going to look after this one.'

Tony took the lamb and held it close. 'Why?' he asked and his eyes were belligerent once more. 'I can look after it. I've already got two at home.'

'That's just it,' Anna said reasonably. 'You've got enough to cope with and you'll be going back to school soon.'

The boy pulled a face but could not argue.

As she stepped off the ladder, the puppy sprang up from his place by the Moses basket, where he had been sleeping, his nose resting on his paws. He galloped across the floor, sliding and tumbling in his anxiety to reach her. He jumped and made little yapping sounds of pleasure.

Anna smiled down at him and fondled him, but her attention was on Tony as she watched him cuddling the newborn lamb. 'They're still your lambs,' she said softly, 'not mine.'

He shrugged and tried to say with grown-up common sense, 'They'll be going for slaughter as soon as they're old enough anyway.' But there was a tremble in his voice that the young boy could not hide. 'Dad always tells me I shouldn't treat them like pets. We're farmers.'

'That's right. Rip's your pet, but—'

'Not really. He's a working dog.' He nodded towards Buster, still jumping and barking excitedly. 'He's growing, isn't he?'

Anna nodded. 'Yes, and he'll be a working dog too, but it doesn't mean I can't fuss him now and then.'

'You'll have to start training him soon, then,' the boy said, knowledgeably.

'I already have.'

Tony's eyes widened. '*You* have? You know about training sheepdogs?'

Suddenly, the wariness was back in Anna's face and she turned away from him. 'A bit,' she said shortly and then deliberately changed the subject. 'Now, we'd better get somewhere sorted out for this little chap to sleep. Let's go and look in the other room.'

They inspected the other upper room together, but both declared it far too cold and draughty for the young lamb.

'We'll all stay in here,' Anna declared. 'And keep each other warm.'

The weather improved at last, the flood waters drained away and Pat Jessop was able to cycle from the village to see Anna. She came up the lane and rode boldly through the farmyard. Leaving her bicycle propped against the barn wall, she took her bag and climbed the track to the top of the rise and down the other side to the cottage.

'I'd like you to see the doctor. Maisie ought to be checked over and you certainly should be.'

'We're all right—' Anna began at once, but Pat interrupted firmly. 'I wouldn't be doing my job properly, love, if I didn't insist. Now, do you want to go into town or have him come here?'

Her eyes wide with fear, the young girl looked around her, as if casting about for some way to escape. 'I—'

'Look,' Pat said gently. 'Why not let Eddie take you

into town next market day? You've got to register the child anyway. You must do that. It's the law.'

'I – I know, but—'

'I'll come with you, if you like.' Pat chuckled. 'I'd quite like a ride in Eddie's old pony and trap again. It wouldn't be the first time.' Her tone grew wistful. 'Mind you, it was a different pony in those days.' Then she became businesslike once more. 'I'll speak to Eddie, and if it's a nice day next Wednesday we'll all go. I'll make an appointment at the doctor's for you and we'll go and see the registrar too.'

There was no getting out of it. When Pat Jessop was in her most persuasive mood, there was no arguing with her.

Anna sighed. 'All right then.'

Pat beamed. 'Good. I shall look forward to our little jaunt. And now I must go. See you next week.'

Pat was already late for her rounds that morning. The cycle ride out to Cackle Hill Farm would put another hour on her routine, but she was not ready to leave yet. There was someone else she wanted to see first.

Pat knocked on the back door of the farmhouse, summoning her most forbidding expression. It was not an easy thing for the district nurse to do, for she was a buxom, pleasant-faced young woman with a ready smile and a teasing, jovial manner. Her long blonde curls were tucked up neatly beneath her cap and the navy blue uniform gave an impression of a severity that was not really part of her nature, though she could, when necessary – as she had been that morning – be firm and persuasive with her patients.

'Oh, it's you,' Bertha said unnecessarily when she opened the door.

'Yes, it's me, Bertha. Can I have a word?'

'What about?'

'Oh things,' Pat said airily evasive. 'How about a cup of tea? I'm parched. It's a long ride out here.'

'It's not a cafe. I haven't time to be making tea.'

'Oh come on, Bertha, there's a dear. Surely, we've known one another long enough—'

'Oh aye, we know enough about each other not to need cosy chats over my kitchen table.'

But seeing that the nurse was not to be budged, Bertha turned away, muttering, 'Oh, come in then, if you must.'

Pat stepped into the warm kitchen, drew off her gloves and held her hands out to the roaring fire in the range. How different was this kitchen to the meagre surroundings in the little white cottage over the hill. Yet Pat could feel that there was already far more love in the tumbledown haven near the woods than there ever would be in this house.

For a brief moment she wondered if Bertha was right. Was there an affair going on between Eddie and the girl? Perhaps the child *was* his. But then she dismissed her fanciful notions as being just that. She had seen them together and whilst there was no doubting Eddie's concern for Anna's welfare, it seemed to be no more than that.

But who knew what the future might bring? For a moment she felt a pang of sympathy for Bertha, who was at this moment banging cups and saucers onto the table with bad grace.

'This is very kind of you, Bertha. It's cold riding

about the countryside on that bike in this weather.' But Pat's words were only greeted with a belligerent glare.

When the tea was ready, they sat down together on opposite sides of the table.

'What is it you want, then? Come to talk me round about that little slut up yonder?' Bertha jerked her head in the direction the cottage lay. ''Cos if you have, you're wasting your time.'

'Not really, Bertha,' Pat said, taking a sip of tea and then placing her cup carefully onto its saucer. She looked up and held Bertha's gaze. 'I just wondered what you know about her.'

Bertha shrugged her fat shoulders. 'Nowt. Nor do I want to.'

'Why not?' Pat's question was direct and pointed.

'Why d'ya think?'

Pat leant ever so slightly towards her. 'I don't know, Bertha. That's why I'm asking you.'

Bertha clattered her own cup into its saucer. 'It's obvious, ain't it? She's Eddie's bit on the side. He's got her into trouble and she's coming knocking at his door. And him being the soft fool he is—'

Pat was shaking her head, unable to believe the tirade of abuse coming out of Bertha's mouth. 'Bertha, your Eddie's not like that.'

'How do you know?' Bertha's retort was like a whiplash. 'Men are all the same. Only after one thing. And even when they've got it on tap at home, it's never enough.' Her small mouth twisted into a bitter sneer.

Pat was appalled at what she was hearing. Eddie's home life must be far worse than she had imagined. Whether or not Eddie had looked for comfort elsewhere, Pat couldn't be sure, but she knew one thing now.

If he had, she wouldn't blame him.

She stood up, unwilling to listen a moment longer to Bertha's twisted logic. The whole village had known for years that Bertha's father had been a 'ladies' man'. Pat had grown up hearing the gossip, witnessing the men's nudges and winks and the women 'tut-tutting' in sympathy with his poor wife. But what she hadn't realized was the terrible effect her father's philandering had had on the young Bertha.

'Do you know something, Bertha? I feel sorry for you. Really I do. But you're a fool. You've got a good man in Eddie Appleyard. There's never been a hint of gossip about him and other women that I've heard. And, believe me, in my job I'd hear it. I carry a lot of secrets for folks round here. And that's what they'll always remain. Secrets. But I'm telling you now, Bertha, Eddie's a good man and I believe him. He felt sorry for that lass and tried to help her.' She leant towards Bertha to emphasize her point. 'And that's all.'

Bertha heaved herself to her feet. 'Get out of my kitchen, Pat Jessop. You're another of his fancy women. Oh, don't think I don't know that you an' him went together afore you found yourself a better catch. And now your husband's dead, you're trying to worm your way back in with Eddie. Well, you won't get the farm. I'll tell you that. I'm his wife and all this' – she waved her arms to encompass the house and all the land that lay around it – 'will one day belong to my son.' She jabbed her finger into her own chest. '*My* son.'

Pat shook her head. 'Oh Bertha,' she said sadly, 'is that all poor Eddie is to you? A good catch?'

Bertha's eyes narrowed. 'I told you, get out of my kitchen, Pat Jessop.'

Pat pedalled away from the farm with a heavy heart.

Poor Eddie, she was thinking. *Poor, poor Eddie. And that poor lass, too*, for she was sure that Bertha Appleyard was just biding her time and that one day, when the opportunity came, she would cause that poor lass a whole barrowload of trouble.

Fourteen

'I don't want to go. I don't see why I have to go.'
Anna's face was mutinous. 'The baby's fine. You've
said so yourself. And so am I. We don't need a doctor.'

Pat was patiently adamant. 'But *I* need you to see a
doctor. If there was anything wrong, then I'd be for the
high jump. You wouldn't want me to lose my job,
would you?'

If Pat had hoped to appeal to Anna's sympathy, she
was sadly mistaken. 'It wouldn't have anything to do
with you. Nobody knows about me. Nobody knows
I'm here.' She paused and, almost accusingly, added,
'Do they?'

'No.' Pat was holding onto her patience. 'But like I
said, if there was anything wrong and you had to see
a doctor – or even go to the hospital – well, questions
would be asked.'

Anna frowned. 'What do you mean "wrong"?'

'I like to have a newborn baby checked thoroughly.
And only a doctor can do that properly. And you
should be checked too, particularly when a doctor
didn't attend the birth.' Pat forbore to add: *Especially
when the birth happened in such a squalid place.*
Instead she added, 'Besides, you've got to register her.'

Anna's frown deepened, but at last she muttered,
'All right, then.'

So on market day the following week Eddie took

Pat, Anna and the child into the market town of Ludthorpe. The baby was snugly wrapped in shawls and her mother held her close for extra warmth.

'We'll have to go in the trap,' Eddie had said. 'I've got to save me petrol for the tractor.'

Above the rattle of the wheels, Pat chattered merrily.

'This is a treat and no mistake. I can get some shopping that I can't manage on my bicycle.' She smiled saucily at Eddie. 'We'll have to do this more often, Eddie.'

He smiled, but did not answer her.

From the moment they had climbed into the trap outside the white cottage, Anna had seemed ill at ease. As they came down the hill towards the church with its tall spire and turned right along a street that widened out into the marketplace, Pat noticed that the girl's nervousness was increasing. Her eyes were wide and dark with fear and her hands trembled. They passed through the busy marketplace and in front of the low, whitewashed Shepherd's Crook. Eddie glanced at it with nostalgia. He'd had some good times in there. He'd had some good pals and he missed their friendly company on market days, but he had kept his vow. He would never again get sow drunk.

Pat put her arm around Anna's shoulders. 'It's all right, love. I'll come in with you, if you want me to.' With kindly bluntness, she added, 'You're not the first to have a bairn with no dad around and you'll not be the last neither. There's just one thing, though. You do know that you can't put the father's name on the birth certificate when you're not married.' She leant a little closer. 'I presume you're not married to the father, are you?'

Anna shook her head with a vehemence that sur-

126

prised both Pat and Eddie, who was listening. 'No,' the girl almost spat. 'No, I'm not.'

'Well then,' Pat went on placidly, giving no sign that she had noticed the girl's agitation, 'in that case, you have to register the child in your surname. That's all.'

'I – know,' the girl whispered, but Pat could see that she was still disturbed.

'Mr Bowen's not going to judge you. He's just there to do his job.'

Anna hung her head, her dark hair falling down like curtains on either side of her face, hiding her expression. Above her bent head, Pat and Eddie exchanged an anxious glance. Then Pat pulled a face and lifted her shoulders in a gesture of bewilderment.

When Eddie pulled the trap to a halt outside a tall, stone-clad building with pillars on either side of the huge oak door, Anna was still white-faced and trembling. When she walked into the registrar's dingy office, she almost turned and ran.

'Go on, love. It'll be all right.' Pat gave her a gentle push. 'I'll be just out here if you need me.'

Mr Reginald Bowen was a bent, wizened little man with a wrinkled, unsmiling face. He frowned at her over small, steel-rimmed spectacles and his beady eyes seemed to bore into her soul. She felt that he could read her innermost secrets.

But Anna's first impression was wrong. When the registrar spoke, his voice was gentle. When he moved forward and ushered her to a seat in front of his desk, his manner was kind. As she sat down, Anna looked into his face, close to her now as he bent forward and, with a hooked finger, gently pulled aside the shawl so that he might see the child.

'So this is your little one.' Mr Bowen smiled and all

the deep lines on his face seemed to curve upwards so that his whole face seemed to be smiling. His beady eyes were no longer fearsome, but twinkled with pleasure. 'What a little treasure. A girl, is it?'

Anna nodded.

'Well now.' Mr Bowen straightened up and went round to his own side of the desk. He pulled a notepad towards him and, pen poised, glanced up at her. His 'official' face returned and he looked severe once more. Anna was still a little nervous, but no longer frightened of what she must do. It had to be done, for the sake of her child.

'I must ask you a lot of questions,' the registrar explained, 'but I want to reassure you that whatever you tell me is in the strictest confidence.'

Anna bit her lip and nodded.

'There now, shall we begin?'

The child's Christian name, date and place of birth were quite easy to answer, but when it came to Anna's details she hesitated and bit her lip. Mr Bowen glanced up.

'Don't be shy, my dear. I can assure you that nothing can shock me. I've seen and heard it all.'

Have you? Anna wanted to cry. *Is there no story you could hear that wouldn't shock and disgust you? Perhaps if you heard what happened to me . . .?*

Softly, Mr Bowen interrupted her thoughts. 'I take it you're not married?'

Anna shook her head.

'Then we must register your little girl under your surname. We cannot put the father's name on the certificate unless he is here. Are you in touch with the father? Could he – er – be persuaded to come with you?'

Harshly, Anna said, 'I don't want his name on it.'

'I see,' the man said. He cleared his throat and added, 'Have you any identification with you? Your own birth certificate?'

Again, Anna answered with a mute shake of her head.

'Your identity card then or your ration book?'

He bent his head, preparing to write again, but when she did not speak, he looked up once more. Anna was staring at him, her face devoid of colour. Nervously, she ran her tongue around her mouth to moisten her dry lips.

'Y-yes,' she stammered as, with a trembling hand, she pulled the documents from her pocket and held them out to him.

'Ah,' Mr Bowen said as he perused the papers. 'Woods. I see your name is Annabel Woods.'

Anna nodded. Hoarsely, almost as if she were dragging out the words, she said, 'But – but I'm called Anna.'

'Well, that seems to be in order, my dear,' Mr Bowen said, handing the documents back. Anna almost snatched the card and book from his fingers and pushed them deep into her coat pocket.

'So now we can register your little one. Maisie Woods? Is that it? No second name?'

Anna stared at him for a moment and then said slowly, 'Yes. Maisie Patricia. After Mrs Jessop. She's been – very kind.'

Mr Bowen smiled and, for the first time, Anna understood the expression 'wreathed in smiles'. All the lines in his face seemed to join together in one huge smile. 'She's a lovely lady. She'll be tickled pink.'

*

Registering both herself and her child at the doctor's surgery was easy, especially as now she had Pat's comforting presence beside her. The receptionist accepted their names as Annabel and Maisie Patricia Woods. Only one moment gave Anna a brief scare.

'We might need to see your birth certificates at some point,' the woman said, 'but it doesn't matter today.'

Anna breathed again. She turned to Pat, who was now standing by her side. 'I hope you don't mind. I called her after you.'

'Oh ducky . . .' Pat said and squeezed her arm. As Mr Bowen had predicted, Pat really did turn pink with pleasure.

The doctor was young, a junior partner in the well-established practice in Ludthorpe.

'I think you'll get on better with Dr Mortimer,' Pat had told her. 'Dr Jacobs is an old dear, but a bit crusty, if you know what I mean. He's an ex-army doctor and not ever so good with babies and children. He's a big man and his handlebar moustache frightens the little ones.' Pat laughed merrily. 'And the not-so-little ones sometimes, too. But Dr Mortimer's a dear.'

The young man's fresh face beamed as Pat ushered a nervous Anna into the surgery. He bounced up from his chair and sprang around the desk to shake Pat's hand. 'Nurse Jessop. Lovely to see you. Come in, come in. How kind of you to bring me a new patient.' And he smiled at Anna and held out his arms to take her baby. 'Now, let's have a look at little Maisie, shall we?'

Swiftly and expertly, he examined the baby, taking time to murmur endearments to her and even to tickle and play with her so that he gained her confidence. 'Well, she's fine,' he said straightening up at last. He turned towards Anna. 'And how's the new mother coping? Any problems.'

Anna bit her lip, glanced nervously at Pat and then shook her head.

'I need to examine you, Mrs Woods. If you like to undress behind the curtains and then—'

'No!'

There was a startled silence and Pat looked up from where she was redressing the baby. 'It's all right, Anna. I'll be here.'

Avoiding their glances, Anna shook her head. 'I'm fine. I don't mind you looking at the baby, but I don't need—'

'It really is advisable, Mrs Woods—'

'Stop calling me Mrs Woods,' Anna snapped. 'It's Miss—'

There was an awkward silence and then, to their horror, Anna burst into tears. 'I'm so sorry. I – I didn't mean to be rude. It's just – I'm so frightened.'

'Frightened?' The young doctor was genuinely distressed. 'Of me?'

Anna's voice was muffled by her tears, but they both heard her whisper, 'Of you touching me.'

Again, the doctor and Pat Jessop exchanged a glance. A look that said: *There's something going on here that we don't know about.*

'I'll be right with you, love,' Pat tried to reassure her. 'I'll even hold your hand, but the doctor must examine you internally to make sure—'

'Internally?' Anna almost shrieked. 'Whatever for?'

'To make sure everything's as it should be. It is important both for now and for the next time you have a child—'

'There won't be a next time,' Anna interrupted bitterly. 'I'll make sure of that.'

Again a look passed between the doctor and the district nurse, but neither of them said anything.

After a great deal of gentle persuasion, for both doctor and nurse could see that the girl was genuinely terrified, Anna gave her reluctant consent. The examination was difficult. Despite the doctor telling her to relax, Anna tensed every muscle against him. But at last he said, 'Everything seems to be fine.' He could not stop himself adding, 'Physically.'

Anna took no notice and pulled on her clothes quickly, but Pat gave a little nod of agreement.

There was something upsetting this poor girl and she meant to find out what it was. She had grown fond of Anna and she could understand now why the kindly Eddie Appleyard was still taking such risks to help her. There was just something about the girl. Even Pat couldn't put her finger on quite what it was. Anna was a strange mixture of vulnerability and feistiness. *But for some reason*, Pat thought, *she makes you want to put your arm round her and take care of her*.

Pat acted out the thought, putting her arm about the girl's shoulders. 'Let's get you home now. Eddie'll be waiting and, if I know babies, it won't be long before Maisie here starts to let us know she's hungry.'

As she led the girl from the room, Pat glanced back over her shoulder. 'Thank you very much, Dr Mortimer.' She gave a brief nod to the young doctor that said silently: *I'll look after her*.

The doctor smiled but his glance, following the young girl, was full of concern. He wished the girl would stay, would allow him more time to talk to her. He was sure she needed help. He knew he could give it.

But it was obvious she couldn't wait to get away from his surgery. The young man sighed as he promised himself that the next time he saw Nurse Jessop on her own, he would ask her about the mysterious Anna Woods.

'You're home from market early. Couldn't ya find a doxy today?' Bertha paused significantly. 'Or don't ya need one now you've got a live-in trollop just over the hill?'

Eddie had dropped Anna and the child off at the end of the track on the far side of the wood.

'Are you sure it's not too far for you, lass? Carrying the little 'un an' all?' he'd asked, but Anna had shaken her head. 'It'll do me good.'

'I know of someone who's not likely to need their pram any more. I'll see if I can get it for you,' Pat offered.

'I can't pay for it—' Anna began, but Pat laughed. 'It's had seven bairns in it. It's that battered I don't reckon Mrs Dawson'll want anything for it.' Hastily, before Anna might think she was being treated like a charity case, the district nurse added, 'But I'll ask her. We'll do it proper.' Pat waved. 'See you soon, love. Now, Eddie, you'd best get me home. I've still got patients I must see today.'

How different was Pat's attitude towards the young lass, Eddie was thinking now as he faced his wife. He couldn't help comparing the fat, blowsy woman before him, with her small, mean mouth and beady, suspicious eyes, with Pat's warm friendliness and ready laugh.

For once his anger bubbled to the surface. 'Give it a rest, Bertha,' he snapped. He spun round and left the house, slamming the back door behind him.

So, Bertha thought, her eyes narrowing, *I was right. That little trollop is still in the cottage. Well, Mr Eddie Appleyard, we'll have to see about that, won't we? But I'm patient. I can wait. I can bide me time. I can wait years, if that's what it takes. But one day, oh yes, one day. There's summat funny going on there with that little madam and one day I'll find out what it is.*

Fifteen

By the time the snow and the flood waters were gone, Anna had begun to feel a little safer in her hideaway home. Until Joe Wainwright arrived to repair the roof.

Anna saw a lorry chugging towards her down the track from the farm. At first she thought it was Eddie, but as the vehicle drew nearer she realized that the driver was a stranger.

The lorry halted in front of the cottage and now Anna could see the name painted along the side. *Joe Wainwright, Builder.*

The man climbed stiffly out of the cab. He was small and stocky and dressed in corduroy trousers and jacket with a red neckerchief tucked into his striped shirt. He was very bow-legged and walked with a rolling gait as he came towards her, holding out his callused hand in greeting. His face, with three or four days' growth of stubble, was swarthy and lined. Anna couldn't help staring at him as she put out her hand, a little nervously, to shake his.

Joe laughed. 'Aye, I know I'm a funny little feller. I couldn't stop a pig in a passage, could I, lass? But I'm good at me job, else Eddie wouldn't have asked me to come and look at that there roof.'

He squinted up at the holes in the thatch. 'Aye, that's no problem. We'll soon have you all shipshape, lass.' His glance rested on her once more. He gave a little nod. 'So you're the one all the village is talking about, a' ya? The one Eddie Appleyard's moved into his cottage? A bonny 'un an' all.' Joe looked around him, his sharp eyes searching. 'And ya've a babby, ain't ya?'

Anna felt a prickle of fear. It was the first time her privacy had been invaded so boldly. Pat's questioning had been probing, certainly, but it had been done with a feeling of genuine concern. This man was just plain nosy.

'I have,' Anna said shortly. 'But it's not Mr Appleyard's bairn, if that's what folks are saying.'

Unabashed, Joe wheezed with laughter. With blunt honesty, he said, 'Aye well, lass, that's what they *are* saying.' He winked. 'You should hear the owd beezums in the village. Clackety-clack, their tongues are going. Like me to set 'em straight, would ya?'

Anna shrugged. 'I don't care one way or the other. *I* know the truth and so does Mr Appleyard.'

She wondered how the village had heard of her existence in the secluded, tumbledown cottage. Her mouth tightened involuntarily. There was only one person, other than the Appleyard family, who knew she was here. Pat Jessop. And to think Anna had allowed herself to trust the nurse.

Joe interrupted her thoughts. 'Aye, but his *wife* dun't, does she?'

Incredulous, Anna stared at him. 'Are you telling me that it's her spreading the gossip?'

He rubbed his fingers on the bristly growth on his chin. 'Well, who else could it be? No one else knew you was here. 'Cept their lad, Tony.' He gave another wheezing laugh. 'And I don't reckon it's the sort of thing he'd tell his schoolmates, do you?'

Anna chastised herself inwardly. She had been wrong

to accuse Pat. Thank goodness it had only been in her mind and not spoken aloud.

'Where've you come from then?' Joe's prying was not finished.

'That's my business,' Anna snapped, hoping that she could offend him just enough to stop his questions but not enough to prevent him mending the roof. But it was impossible to offend Joe Wainwright. His skin was as thick and impervious as the leather on his boots. He just laughed and countered with another question. 'And are you staying here then?'

'Not for long. Now,' she added, trying desperately to steer the focus of his attention away from her, 'would you like a cup of tea and a slice of currant cake? I've just managed to master the bread oven.'

'I wouldn't say no, lass. I wouldn't say no.'

Joe Wainwright was, as he had said, good at his work. In a few hours the thatched roof was repaired.

As he climbed down his ladder, he remarked, 'I see you've had a bit o' trouble with that there wall. Eddie mend that himself, did he?'

'Yes.'

'Ah well, 'spect he has to watch the pennies like the rest of us. Specially with Bertha Tinker for a wife.' He sniffed contemptuously. 'By, she's a shrew and no mistake. Just like 'er mother. No wonder poor old Wilf Tinker used to look elsewhere for 'is comforts.' He gave a huge wink and tapped the side of his nose as he added, 'If ya know what I mean.'

For once, Anna could not stop a twinge of curiosity. She did not venture any questions, but Joe needed no prompting and she made no attempt to stop him. 'Mind you,' he went on, warming to his subject as he found a new ear to listen to his gossip, 'he's a bit of a lad in more ways than one, is Wilf. Ended up in the nick, he has.'

Anna's eyes widened, but still she ventured no comment.

'Aye, black market in the war, y'know.'

Anna bit her lip.

'Course, lots o' folk dabbled a bit in a harmless sort of way. Most of us got away wi' it.' He winked again, indicating that he, Joe Wainwright, had not been above making a bit on the side. 'But poor old Wilf Tinker was 'is own worst enemy. Couldn't tell a lie, see. Not a convincing one at any rate and o' course when he was faced with the law . . .' He shrugged and spread his hands. 'They saw right through 'im. Pity, really. He's not a bad sort in lots of ways. He certainly wasn't a real crook, if you knows what I mean.' He nodded knowingly. 'There was some hard nuts in the war, lass. Real spiv types that'd sell their granny if they thought they could get a bob or two for her.'

A shudder ran through Anna and she felt suddenly sick. She turned her head away before Joe should read her expression.

'And this Wilf Tinker was Mrs Appleyard's father?' she asked, recovering herself.

'Tha's right. Him and his missis had two lasses. Bertha and Lucy. Lucy did well for herself. Married an office worker and lives in Ludthorpe. Quite the lady, Lucy is. I reckon poor old Bertha envies her. Though give me Eddie Appleyard any time. He's all right, is Eddie. But I dun't reckon I need to tell you that, lass, do I?'

Anna turned back slowly to meet his steady gaze. 'No, Mr Wainwright,' she said. 'You don't.'

By shearing time Maisie was out in the bright, early summer days, sitting up in the deep, black pram that Pat had brought for her.

'Jessie Dawson doesn't want owt for it.'

Anna had eyed the district nurse sceptically. 'Are you sure?'

'Course I am.' Pat laughed. 'Mind you, I had a job to get her to part with it. She shed tears as I wheeled it away. "All my bairns have been in that pram," she said.'

Anna frowned. 'Are you sure she won't want it again? I mean, she sounds very fond of children. She might—'

'I'm sure Jessie'd love another half-dozen given the chance. But she won't have the chance, love. She had to have a hysterectomy after the last baby.'

Anna put her hand onto the well-worn handle. The pram sagged down at one corner where a spring had weakened.

'It's a bit battered, ducky, like I told you.'

'It's fine.' Anna smiled as she rocked the pram gently. 'Maisie will love being outside.'

The local farmers all helped one another at certain times of the year: haymaking, harvest and, for those who kept sheep on the Wolds' hills, shearing. But with Eddie's small flock, only Sam Granger, an acknowledged 'dab hand' at shearing, would come. And, of course, Joe Wainwright, who seemed to turn up at every event, would no doubt be there.

On the day before shearing was to begin in the yard at Cackle Hill Farm, Anna wheeled Maisie into the warm sunshine and parked the pram just outside the gate in the fence surrounding their home. She glanced back towards the cottage garden with a small stab of pride. Despite her intention to leave as soon as she could, she had not been able to stand the sight of the neglected garden. In front of the cottage, she had scythed the small patches of grass and was able to keep it short now with a battered old lawnmower that Pat had brought her.

'I've treated myself to a brand-new one,' the nurse had said, beaming. 'I've got quite a big lawn and this one was too much like hard work. But you're young and strong. You'll cope with it.'

Anna had weeded the flowerbeds and now Canterbury bells, cornflowers and convolvulus sprouted happily, whilst lupins and irises were just coming into flower. At the side of the building, there had once been a square of kitchen garden. Whilst Anna was adamant that she would not be here long enough to enjoy the fruits of her labour, she had nevertheless cleared the ground and planted onions and lettuce.

'Why don't you plant cabbage and caulis?' Eddie had suggested in March. 'And what about runner beans and . . .'

'It's not worth it,' Anna said quietly. 'I won't be here to enjoy them.'

Eddie's face fell.

'Unless you'd like me to plant them for you?' she added.

Eddie shook his head. 'No, lass,' he said heavily as he turned away. 'Don't bother.'

But she had dug the kitchen garden over anyway and

now, unearthed from the choking weeds and nettles, a rhubarb plant flourished in one corner flanked by two gooseberry bushes.

Buster, usually so boisterous, sat by the pram whenever Maisie was outside, as if guarding the child. Today, however, Anna had other work for him.

The sheep had all been washed in the stream a few days earlier in time for their fleeces to dry in the summer sunshine. It had been hard work, for the sheep hated being plunged into the water and had fought and struggled. Panting and soaked through, Anna and Eddie had laughed at each other.

'You look like a drowned rat,' she had giggled.

'So do you,' he had countered, grinning. 'Go on home. Go and get dry.'

'Why don't you come too? There's a sharp breeze. You'll be chilled by the time you walk back to the farm.'

'Aye, mebbe you're right.'

They walked together towards the cottage, Eddie pushing the pram containing a sleeping Maisie.

'D'you know,' he mused. 'I don't reckon I ever pushed our Tony in his pram. Not once.'

Anna laughed softly. 'Not reckoned to be man's work, eh?'

'Wouldn't have bothered me,' Eddie said and there was a note of regret in his tone as if he thought he might have missed a special moment.

As he manoeuvred the pram through the back door, Anna said, 'I'll get a blanket for you. Could you set up the clothes airer? And get those wet things off.'

Eddie grinned. 'Yes, ma'am.'

Anna changed into dry clothes in her bedroom and Eddie sat wrapped in a blanket whilst his wet garments steamed in front of the fire. Anna handed him a cup of hot cocoa and sat down beside him.

'A good job done.' She smiled.

Eddie glanced up to meet her eyes. As he took the cup, their fingers touched briefly. 'Aye lass,' he said. 'A good job done.'

They sat together in companionable silence and even when his clothes were dry enough to put on Eddie seemed reluctant to leave.

He paused in the doorway on his way out and said softly, 'Thanks, lass, for everything.' Very gently, he touched her cheek and then turned and walked away up the slope.

'Oh, Eddie, what a lovely man you are,' Anna whispered to herself as she watched him go. For the first time in many months she suddenly realized that she had not been afraid to be alone with a man.

And now the day for shearing was almost here. Anna surveyed the sheep contentedly grazing in the field near her cottage. Then she shaded her eyes and looked up to the top of the rise, where she could see Tony standing looking down the track towards her. Rip was sitting obediently beside him. She had often seen the two of them at the top of the hill, but not once, since the day he had been sent by his father to fetch her to help with the difficult birth of twin lambs, had the boy visited the cottage.

Now she saw him glance, just once, over his shoulder as if checking to see if anyone was watching him. Then suddenly he launched himself down the hill, running pell-mell towards her, Rip bounding along at his side barking joyfully.

The dog reached her first and jumped up to lick her face. Then Rip capered with the half-grown puppy.

Anna held out her arms and, as Tony flung himself into them, she lifted him bodily off the ground and swung him round.

'Oh, I've missed you,' she said impulsively as she set him on the ground and breathlessly they leant against each other, laughing together. She pulled back and held him at arm's length. 'You've grown. I'm sure you've grown.'

Tony grinned. 'Nah.'

'You have, you have,' she insisted and then laughed again. 'But if you haven't then come and look at Maisie. She certainly has.'

As he reached the pram, Tony gasped. 'Oh. She's sitting up and she's smiling. Really smiling now.' He held out a finger to her. The baby gripped it and tried to pull it towards her mouth, but the boy laughed and gently eased it from her grasp. 'No, no, dirty.'

Maisie blinked at him. Her smile faded. Her chin quivered and she began to whimper, huge tears welling in her dark brown eyes.

'Oh don't. Don't cry, little Maisie. I didn't mean to make you cry, but my finger's mucky.' He leant towards her and tickled Maisie until she chuckled once more.

Watching the young boy's tenderness with her child, Anna felt a lump come to her throat.

'Come on,' she tried to say briskly, though she didn't quite manage it for her voice was unsteady. 'We've work to do.'

Sixteen

'Sam's coming tomorrow to start the shearing,' Tony said. 'And Dad says he wants you to come down to the yard and wrap the fleeces for him.' The boy put his head on one side and regarded her thoughtfully. 'Do you know how to do it?'

Anna closed her eyes for a moment as the memories came flooding back, threatening, not for the first time, to overwhelm her. She knew just how it would be. The yard alive with activity: sheep bleating, men laughing and ribbing one another, yet all the while the fleeces would be falling from the sheep as if by magic under the expert hands wielding the shears. She opened her eyes again, but, not trusting herself to speak, she merely nodded.

'We've to round up about half the flock tomorrow morning. Joe Wainwright comes an' all. He cuts all the clags off and opens up the necks for Sam. We do about half the flock one day and the rest the next.'

'Oh.' Anna raised her eyebrows. 'I'd have thought an expert shearer could do your dad's flock in a day.'

Tony grinned. 'He could easy, but he doesn't start till midday. Ses he likes the sheep to have the sun on their backs for a while. Makes the shearing easier, he ses.'

Anna smiled, for a moment her thoughts were far away once more. 'So it does,' she murmured. 'I'd forgotten that.' Then she brought her wandering mind back to the job in hand. 'So, are you coming to help me round them up in the morning?'

Tony nodded. 'I'll be here early.'

The following morning Anna and Tony worked together, leaving Buster sitting beside the pram. For once, the little dog was restless, wanting to join in the rounding up. At last, unable to sit still any longer, he bounded across to Rip, startling the five sheep the older dog was guiding up the track. Anna and Tony burst out laughing, imagining they could see an aggrieved look on Rip's face.

'Just look at him,' Tony spluttered. 'He looks like me dad when I've done something daft.'

'I know just what you mean. He looks as if he's saying, "Look what you've done. Now I've got to start all over again."'

'And poor Buster hasn't a clue what he *has* done.'

'Here, boy. Here, Buster,' Anna called and the young dog came slowly towards her, head down in apology. But Anna fondled him. 'It's all right, but you've got to learn. Now, stay.'

The dog lay down whilst Anna, holding the crook that Eddie had lent her, moved to the right and began to whistle to Rip. With a series of shouted instructions and whistles, they rounded up the five sheep again.

'Yan, tan, tethera, fethera, pethera . . .' she murmured to herself as her eyes misted over once more. But Tony had heard her.

'Oh, you can count like the shepherds, an' all.'

'What?' Anna turned startled eyes upon him, hardly realizing that she had spoken aloud. 'Oh – er – yes.'

'Then you can teach me. Dad only knows "yan, tan, tethera", then he forgets. How far can you count?'

145

'Only to about twenty . . .'

'That'll do.' Tony grinned.

Anna smiled. 'You follow Rip up the hill and see he gets them into the barn whilst I get the next lot. And I'll try to get this little rascal to do as he's told.' She turned towards the young dog. 'Come on, Buster. High time you learned to earn your keep.'

Anna felt very nervous about going down to the yard. If it hadn't been for the fact that she owed Eddie Appleyard so much, she would have stayed in her little haven, safe from inquisitive eyes. But, she sighed, she had no choice. So she put Maisie in the pram with a bottle for her feed and set off up the track. Joe Wainwright and a man Anna had not met before were already at work in the yard.

Eddie made the brief introduction. 'This is Sam, Anna.' Eddie made no reference to the baby in the pram, which she had parked at the edge of the yard.

'Morning, lass,' Joe greeted her cheerfully, but Sam glowered briefly at her and then turned his back.

As she was making ready the table where she would lay the fleeces to wrap them, Joe came and stood beside her. 'Tek no notice of old Sam, lass. He's got a daughter of his own about your age. And he's a better guard dog than Eddie's sheepdog ovver yonder.' The man gave a wheezing laugh. He leant a little closer. 'Won't let the poor lass even speak to the young fellers, ne'er mind walk out with any of 'em.'

Anna's mouth tightened as she glanced towards Maisie sitting contentedly in her pram. 'He doesn't approve of me, you mean.'

Quite unabashed, Joe nodded. 'Summat like that,

aye, lass. But you mark my words, he's stacking up a barrowload of trouble for 'issen. The more you try to keep 'em tied down, the more they'll try to slip the leash. 'Tis only nature, lass, 'tis only nature.' Joe laughed again and leant closer to whisper, 'But what he forgets is that some of us round here have long memories. When he was a young feller his wife's father went after him with a shotgun one night.'

Anna turned to stare at Joe.

'You've heard of a shotgun wedding, lass, ain't ya?'

Anna nodded.

'Well, that was a real one, an' no mistake, 'cos their first bairn was born only six months after they was wed.' Joe winked and tapped the side of his nose. 'So Sam's the last one to be disapproving, ain't he?'

Anna said nothing, but let her head drop forwards to hide her face. Then she felt Joe's friendly hand rest briefly on her shoulder. 'Chin up, lass. You'm got a lovely babby there. Be proud of her.'

Then he turned and walked away, but the man's bluff kindness had brought tears to her eyes.

The men worked hard, with Anna alongside them pausing only to feed and change Maisie and to grab a quick bite to eat herself. She watched in admiration as Sam tipped each sheep onto its rump. So sharp were his blades and so experienced his hands that he didn't even seem to work the shears, but swept the blades down with long easy strokes, deftly turning the animal so that the fleece came off in one whole piece. Then it was Anna's turn to pick up the fleece and take it to the slatted table. Taking it by the hind legs, she flung it upwards and outwards, as if shaking a rug, so that dust and loose fibres floated around her. Then she picked off all the bits of briar and grass that still clung to it. She folded the flanks towards the centre to form a rectangle and rolled the fleece from the back end up towards the neck, where she drew out the neck wool to form a tie long enough to encircle the rolled fleece and tuck back in under itself.

All afternoon she worked steadily, until Eddie called a halt and Bertha appeared in the yard carrying drinks for the workers. Anna turned away, but not before she had seen the look of fury on the older woman's face.

It was late in the evening when Anna climbed the track wearily, with scarcely the strength left to push the pram up the slope. Even when the shearing was done for the day and the men had gone, the work was not finished. The sheared sheep had to be driven back to the field and the next lot brought down to the farm for the night, ready for shearing the following day.

'Dad, Dad,' Anna heard Tony shouting. 'There's three lambs can't find their mothers. They're crying.'

The high-pitched bleating of the lambs as they darted from one ewe to another, unable to recognize their newly shorn dams, was pitiful. But Eddie only chuckled. 'It's all right, lad, I'll make sure they've found the right ones afore I leave them. But you run on home now. Ya mam'll be wanting you away to your bed. And you too, Anna, you take that little one home. You look all in, ya'sen.'

'Goodnight, then, Eddie. I'll see you in the morning.'

'Goodnight, lass. And thanks for all your help today.'

Anna smiled and turned away. As she entered the cottage, she leant a moment against the closed door, glad to be back in her little sanctuary. And yet it hadn't been a bad day. Despite Sam's obvious disapproval and Bertha's malevolent glare, Joe had treated her kindly. It had been a good day.

There had only been one moment that had caused her anguish, but no one could have guessed. At least, she hoped no one had noticed that for a moment her heart had seemed to rise into her throat and her hands had trembled.

Joe had unwittingly brought about the stab of fear. He had been admiring Sam's skill at shearing and had commented lightly. 'You remind me of a young feller that lives over Lincoln way. By, I've never seen a better shearer in me life. Like a knife through butter, it is, to watch him and he never leaves so much as a nick on the sheep. But blessed if I can remember his name.'

'I bet you mean Jed Rower,' she heard Sam say. 'I saw him at the show one year. You'm right, he's a clever feller . . .' The two men had continued their chatter, whilst Anna froze for a moment and then her heart began to pound. Her hands were trembling as she carried the next fleece to the table, her face flushing bright red. Biting her lip, she tried to concentrate on the wrapping, but she did it so badly that she was obliged to unfold it once more and begin again. No one seemed to notice and gradually her heartbeat returned to normal and she tried to squash the thoughts that mention of the name had evoked.

But now, in the stillness of the cottage, those thoughts refused to be ignored.

I must go, was all she could think of. *I'm still not far enough away. Once the shearing's finished, I must move on.*

Seventeen

'You coming with me into town?' Eddie asked Anna as they stacked the rolled fleeces into the back of his trailer to take into Ludthorpe. She shook her head. 'No – I – er – I've things to do.'

'All right, then, lass. I'll see you later. Anything you want bringing?'

Anna's heart beat a little faster and her hands were clammy. She didn't like deceiving Eddie, who had been so kind to her, but, as soon as he had left the farm heading towards the town, she intended to leave too, but in the opposite direction. She dared not tell him, dared not say goodbye, for she knew he would try to persuade her to stay. And he would probably succeed. She would leave via the village, Anna decided. She would call in to say her farewells to Pat and to leave a message for Eddie with her. She could even write him a note . . .

'We'll have to dip in about a fortnight's time . . .' Eddie was saying as he climbed up onto his tractor.

Startled from her own thoughts, Anna said, 'What? What did you say?'

'I said, we'll have to dip all the sheep in about a fortnight.' He smiled down at her. 'I'll need your help then all right, lass. Tony's not strong enough to manage them when they struggle . . .'

Anna stared up at him. Oh no, it wasn't possible. Quite unaware of her plans, Eddie had innocently presented her with yet another reason for her to stay longer.

'Oh, er, right,' she murmured and silently promised: *Two more weeks, then. Just two more weeks and then we'll go.*

Anna stood at the top of the rise, watching the lorry taking a batch of the lambs to market manoeuvre its way out of the gate of Cackle Hill Farm. Beside her Maisie lay asleep in the depths of the black pram, blissfully unaware of her mother's inner turmoil. The young woman smiled gently, though tears prickled her eyes. She couldn't help it. It was not the way of a true farmer. Though never cruel to any animal, nevertheless proper farmers were unsentimental about the need to slaughter the livestock they had so carefully reared. But Anna had not been able to stop herself becoming fond of the woolly little creatures that gambolled and leapt about in their joy at just being alive.

Once she had known that kind of joy.

Her gaze roamed over the slopes of the surrounding fields, vibrant in their summer colours. Below her in the cottage garden splashes of colour vibrated against the darkness of the trees beyond, stately white foxgloves, purple lupins, and pink petunias and even a few early red roses. She wished she could plant more flowers in front of the cottage and there was room in the vegetable patch at the side to plant potatoes, carrots, beans – enough to provide for herself and Maisie for months. She could make it into a real home. She already had, really. She could be content here, almost happy. Anna bit her lip. But it was futile to make such plans.

She couldn't stay here. They had to move on. It wasn't safe. She must get as far away as possible. There were too many people now who knew she was living here. Pat Bishop, Joe Wainwright, the doctor and the registrar in the town and, more recently, the vet and then the men who had come to help with the shearing. And it had been then that she had realized she was still not far enough away. The list of those who now knew where she was was getting far too long, to say nothing of the gossips in the village who knew all about her presence in Eddie Appleyard's shepherd's cottage, even if they had never seen her. The more who knew, the more likely it was that word might get back . . .

And most dangerous of all was Bertha, whose malevolent gaze seemed to follow her everywhere.

It was time to go. The dipping was done, the lambs all gone. Now would be a good time to leave.

Her mind made up, Anna turned her back on the idyllic scene and determinedly pushed the pram down the rough track towards the cottage that had been her haven for the past few months. She would go, she resolved, and go now before she could change her mind.

Back at the cottage, she began to gather her belongings together, her own and Maisie's clothes and food for the journey, piling them all beside the pram. Then she stood looking down at the heap. There was far too much to fit on the pram. Its already sagging springs would never take the extra weight. And there was too much for her to carry. Maybe if she put some in the pram and made up a kind of bundle she could carry on her back . . .

From outside, the sound of Eddie's tractor came closer.

'Oh no!' Anna breathed and hurried outside to forestall him coming into the cottage. He was back earlier than she had thought. She had taken too long to get ready.

He drew to a halt and switched off the engine. Climbing down, he came towards her, smiling. 'Well, lass, that's another lot gone and I got a good price.' His grin widened. 'I'll be able to give you a bonus on your wages.'

Anna smiled tremulously and walked away from the door, trying to keep a distance between him and her home. But her ruse was not working.

'Where's Maisie?' He moved towards the back door.

'She – she's asleep,' Anna said desperately. 'Don't wake her. She's teething and – and she's not sleeping very well.'

This was not strictly true. The child was indeed teething, but she seemed to be having little trouble.

'She's very lucky,' Pat had told Anna on her last visit, adding with a laugh, 'and so are you. Most kiddies have an awful time and so do their mothers. Being kept awake half the night isn't any fun for baby or mother.'

'Oh.' Eddie stopped at once. 'Poor little mite,' he said sympathetically. 'I remember Tony crying a lot when he was teething. I used to rub a little whisky onto his gums.' He grinned. 'But don't tell Pat I told you that, will ya?'

Anna tried to smile, but it was a nervous, half-hearted effort. Eddie didn't seem to notice. His gaze

153

was roving over the outside walls of the cottage. 'You know, this could do with a lick of lime wash—'

At that moment, much to Anna's chagrin, they heard Maisie wail.

Eddie's face brightened. 'She's awake. Now I can see her.' He was in through the back door before Anna could stop him.

She sighed and followed him. He was standing quite still, staring down at the pile of their belongings beside the pram. Slowly he turned to look at Anna, disappointment and concern on his face.

'What's this? You – you're not thinking of leaving, love, are you?'

Silently, Anna nodded.

'Aw, lass, why? What's wrong? Is there something you need? What is it? Tell me and I'll get it.'

Anna shook her head. 'It – it's not that, Eddie. You've been wonderful, so good. Too good—'

He stared at her for a moment and then closed his eyes and groaned. 'Aw, lass, you're not thinking I'm going to want summat in return. Aw, lass, don't ever think that. Not of me.'

'No, no, Eddie,' she reassured him swiftly. 'It's not that. Truly. That – that never entered my head.'

He eyed her sceptically. 'Didn't it?' he asked gently. ''Cos it has into other folks' nasty minds.' His voice dropped to a whisper. 'Even me own wife's.'

'Well, maybe at first,' Anna admitted. 'But not now. Not since I've got to know you. You're just a very kind man, Eddie Appleyard.'

For a moment there was silence between them as they gazed at each other. At last Eddie cleared his throat, but his voice was still husky with emotion as he asked, 'Then why, lass?'

154

Maisie's wailing grew louder and before she answered him, Anna moved to the pram and picked up the child. Resting her baby against her shoulder, Anna patted her back soothingly. Maisie's cries subsided to gentle hiccuping.

'I have to move on. I have to get further away.'

'Why? What is it you're afraid of? *Who* are you afraid of? You've been here months now and no one's come looking for you. Or has summat happened I don't know about?'

Anna lowered her eyes, not daring to meet his steady gaze. Hating herself for lying, she shook her head.

'Then why, lass? You're safe here.' When she did not answer, he added, 'Aren't you?'

Anna closed her eyes and let out a deep sigh. Flatly, she said, 'I don't know. I – I just feel that the further away the better.'

'Further away from where exactly?' Again there was no reply from her, so he prompted gently. 'Won't you trust me enough to tell me that at least?'

In a husky, reluctant whisper she said, 'Lincoln.'

'Lincoln?' Eddie almost laughed. 'Why, that's miles away. No one's going to find you here. To folks from the city, this is the back of beyond.'

Anna smiled thinly but said nothing.

'So will you stay, lass? At least a little longer? It'll be haymaking afore we know it and then harvest . . .'

'And then it'll be winter and I won't be able to go,' she said.

Eddie grinned ruefully. 'Aye, so it will, lass. So it will. You see right through me, don't ya?' They smiled, understanding one another. 'So, will you stay, love? Please say you will.'

With a jolt Anna saw that there were tears in his

eyes. A lump grew in her own throat so that she could not answer. Instead, slowly, she nodded.

Anna and her daughter were still there through hay-making and into the harvest in the heat of August. It seemed as if half the village turned out to help the local farmers get in the harvest.

'It's always happened round here. It's a sort of custom, but more so in the war,' Pat told her. 'With a lot of the fellers away, we had Land Army girls here and the local women helped an' all.' She laughed. 'I reckon we all got to enjoy it.'

'Did – did Eddie have Land Army girls here?' Anna asked.

'Oh yes,' Pat said. 'Most of the farmers did. Some of the girls even stayed on. One girl married a local lad and stayed.' She nodded towards a pretty, fair-haired girl. 'That's her. That's Phyllis. Nice lass, she is. You'd like her. Why don't you let me introduce—'

'No,' Anna said swiftly. 'No, thanks.'

Puzzled, Pat glanced at Anna but said no more. Anna was staring across at Phyllis, almost as if she recognized her and yet she had refused to meet her. In fact, she refused to meet anyone, refused even to try to make friends. Pat sighed. Anna was a funny lass and no mistake.

As Eddie towed the last of the wagons behind the tractor to his stack yard, Pat said, 'There, that's Eddie's all safely gathered in. We've just Ted Bucknall's to do now and that's the harvest home. There'll be a harvest supper in the village hall then. You'll come, won't you?'

Anna shook her head.

'But everyone will be there—'

'No!' Anna was adamant. 'I – I can't.'

Pat sighed as they walked together back towards the farm. 'You will have to mix with folk sometime, love. You can't keep yourself a recluse.' She laughed and nudged Anna's arm. 'They'll be calling you a witch soon.'

Anna smiled wanly.

'And what about Maisie? She needs to play—'

'I play with her.'

'But she needs to be with kiddies of her own age. She needs—'

Anna stopped and turned to face Pat. 'I know you mean it kindly, and I'm grateful, really I am, but I can't mix with folk. And – and I can't let Maisie either.'

'She'll have to when she gets to five years old and has to go to school,' Pat said bluntly. 'You've got to face that, Anna, because it's a fact and you can't get away from it.'

Now Anna smiled. 'I know that, but we'll be miles away from here by then.'

On the evening of the harvest supper, Anna sat alone on the grass outside the little white cottage, watching the sunset. She drew her knees up, wrapped her arms around her legs and rested her chin on her knees. It was so quiet, so still, so peaceful . . .

As the sun dropped lower, emblazoning the western sky with red and gold, Anna dared to feel happy for the first time. The feeling of contentment came stealthily, unbidden, and yet she hardly dared to acknowledge it, to believe that she could ever feel secure and . . .

She heard a movement and jumped, glancing round to see Eddie standing only a few feet from her.

'Sorry, lass,' he said softly. 'I didn't mean to startle you.'

He came across the grass and sat down beside her. 'Lovely sight, ain't it? A Lincolnshire sunset. Nowt to beat it. "Red sky at night, shepherds' delight".'

They sat in companionable silence. For a while, it seemed as if there was no one in the world but them. Then, quietly, Eddie began to talk. 'You must wonder why me an' Bertha ever came to get married.'

'It's not my business, Eddie,' Anna said, not sure she wanted to be the keeper of his confidence. It bound them even closer.

'You might have guessed' – he smiled ruefully – 'that once upon a time I carried a torch for Pat Anderson. Sorry, Jessop she is now.'

'I could see there was a closeness between you,' Anna murmured.

Eddie sighed. 'But she left the village. Went to be a nurse in Ludthorpe and met this handsome young feller at the hospital.' There was no bitterness or jealousy in Eddie's tone, just sadness. 'Couldn't blame her, I suppose. He was a really nice feller.'

'And you started seeing Bertha?'

Eddie gave a short laugh. 'Sort of. She came to work here at the farm. My mam and dad were still alive then, but getting on a bit. Mam needed help in the house and with the dairy work. She was a kindly old dear, my mam.'

'That doesn't surprise me,' Anna said, before she could stop herself.

His eyebrows raised in question, Eddie glanced at her. Anna laughed softly. 'You must take after her, Eddie.'

He smiled and gave a little nod. 'I'd like to think so.' He paused as if lost in thought for a moment. 'Anyway, me mam felt sorry for the Tinker family, specially the youngsters, and when Bertha left school she offered her a job here. And, of course,' he added pointedly as if it explained everything, 'she lived in.'

Anna could imagine how it must have been. A young man, disappointed in love, and a young girl thrown together. Maybe, then, Bertha had been prettier than she was now. Maybe she had fallen in love with Eddie . . .

But Eddie had no such illusions. His next words dispelled Anna's romantic hopes. 'The Tinkers always had an eye for the main chance and my dear wife was no exception. She set her cap at me and I, like a fool, fell for it.' He sighed heavily. 'It wasn't so bad in the early days, I have to admit. She was good to me mam and dad, nursing them in their final illnesses. I'll give her that. But then, after Tony was born, it was as if she gave all the love she had to give to him. So' – he turned to look at her gravely – 'don't ever think, lass, that it's you who's caused trouble between us, 'cos it ain't.'

'I'm very sorry, Eddie,' Anna said huskily. 'There's no happy endings in real life are there? That only happens in books.'

'Don't say that, lass. Mebbe there's not one for me, but for you—'

Anna pursed her mouth and shook her head emphatically. 'No. Not for me either.'

There was a long silence until Eddie said, 'Then I'm sorry too, love. Very sorry.' He paused again before asking tentatively, 'Won't you tell me what happened to you?'

Anna's head dropped forward and she pulled at the grass with agitated fingers. 'I can't. It's – it's too painful.'

'All right, love. But if you ever feel the need to talk, I'm here. I'll always be here for you.'

As if pulled by an invisible string, they turned to look at each other. Hesitantly, Eddie reached out. For a moment, Anna drew in a breath and almost jerked away, but then, seeing the tenderness in his eyes, she allowed him to touch her. He traced the line of her cheek with his roughened forefinger, yet his touch was surprisingly gentle.

'Ya won't leave, lass, will ya?' he pleaded softly. 'Ya'll stay here. With me.'

His face was soft in the golden glow of the sunset, his eyes dark unreadable depths, but she could hear the longing in his voice. Anna trembled. By going, she would hurt this lovely man. This man who had given her everything, yet asked nothing in return. But by staying she risked the safety of herself and her child too.

'Till spring, Eddie,' she whispered. 'That's all I can promise. Till spring.'

Eighteen

Anna did not leave the following spring. Maisie learned to walk on the soft grass of Eddie's meadows on the hillside outside the cottage, whilst Anna helped again with the birthing and rearing of the lambs. Anna planted vegetables in the garden at the back of their home and Eddie renovated the upstairs rooms.

'Maisie needs a room of her own, now she's getting such a big girl,' he said, smiling down at the little girl, who followed him whenever she could, clinging to his legs and gazing up at him. He ruffled her coppery curls and tickled her cheek.

'Tony?' Maisie would ask day after day and Eddie would laugh. 'He's at school, lovey. You'll have to make do with old Eddie today. I know, you can come and watch me do the milking.'

'No, Eddie. She's not to go to the farm,' Anna said, overhearing.

In the past year, she had seen Bertha rarely and, in all that time, had never spoken to her once. The other woman made no trouble now, but on the odd occasions that Eddie had needed Anna's help in the buildings or the yard near the house Anna had felt Bertha's malevolent glare following her.

'It'll be all right—'

'No!' Anna was adamant. 'She's not to go to the farm. Not ever.'

'Bertha wouldn't hurt her, Anna. She's got a lot of faults, but she'd never hurt a child. She loves children.'

'Even *my* child?'

'Oh Anna.' His eyes reproached her. 'She's not a bad woman. She'd not harm your little girl.' He shrugged. 'She didn't like the idea of you being here. Still doesn't, I expect.' He wrinkled his forehead. 'But she's not even mentioned you recently. 'Spect she's got used to you being here now.'

'She doesn't allow Tony to come to see us though, does she?'

Eddie smiled. 'No, but he comes anyway.'

'Not so often now and when he does he comes round by the road and the woods so that she can't see him come up the track.'

'Aye, well, I expect he's only trying to save her feelings. He's very fond of his mam, y'know.'

'Of course he is,' Anna murmured and there was a catch to her voice that Eddie couldn't fail to hear. For a brief moment, her eyes had that haunted, faraway look. 'That's as it should be.' She paused and then added emphatically, 'I'm sorry, but I don't want her to go to the farm.'

Eddie sighed and shrugged. 'All right, love, if that's the way you want it.'

He patted the little girl's head and gently disentangled himself from her clinging arms. 'Ta-ta, lovey,' he murmured and then walked away from them.

Anna bit her lip. He was disappointed, she could see that, but she dared not risk Maisie going to the farm.

She could not blot out the memory of the murderous look in Bertha's eyes at the time of Maisie's birth.

*

They were still living in the cottage when Maisie reached her fourth birthday. And on that day the little girl decided it was high time she investigated what lay beyond the hill up the track from her home. By now Maisie, with her shining coppery curls and dark brown eyes, was bright, intelligent and surprisingly knowledgeable for her age, considering that she had had little contact with the world outside her isolated home.

She knew very few people other than her mother, Eddie, Tony and Pat Jessop. But now the inquisitive child was set on adventure.

'I need to fetch some water,' Anna said. 'Are you coming?'

Maisie shook her head. 'No. I'll stay with Buster.' The dog was now fully trained as a sheepdog and was every bit as trustworthy at looking after the child as he was at guarding Eddie's flock.

Anna shrugged and set off carrying two water buckets. With narrowed eyes Maisie watched her go. When her mother was some distance away, the child went round the side of the cottage and began to climb the hill, hidden from her mother's view if she happened to glance back.

Sensing that his charge was about to do something wrong, Buster began to bark.

'Ssh,' Maisie frowned at him. 'If you make a noise, I'll shut you in the house.'

The dog whined and then leapt around her, trying to shepherd her back home as he would have done a wayward sheep. But the little girl was not as docile as the animals. She wagged her finger at him. 'Quiet, Buster.' Then she added, 'Down!' in such a firm, grown-up voice that the dog obeyed her. Panting, his pink tongue lolling, he watched her climb the hill with anxiety in his eyes. He sensed this was wrong, but he didn't know how to stop her.

At the top of the track, the child, a tiny figure now, looked back. The dog barked and stood up, but Maisie's shrill voice bounced over the breeze to him. 'Stay!' Buster obeyed, though as she disappeared over the brow of the rise he whined unhappily.

The day was bright but cold and blustery and now, in the late afternoon of the February day, Anna sat down for a few moments on an old tree stump near the stream. She looked down into the brook as it bubbled and chattered its way down the slope, past the wood and under the bridge in the lane and on out of sight. Where it went she didn't know, but she felt as if this little stretch of the stream belonged to her. She pulled her coat around her as she watched the bright water. She sighed. She loved this place and now she would hate to leave, but soon they must. This time next year Maisie would be five and, if they stayed, she would have to go to the village school.

Anna couldn't risk it. She would have to get further away. She couldn't risk even more people knowing them. People who might ask questions: teachers, other children and their parents.

She must get away, yet the thought made her feel sad. She stood up, but then, hearing the sound of a bus coming along the lane, she crouched down behind the tree stump until it had passed by. The vehicle stopped and she heard voices. As the bus drew away, she peeped round the side of the stump to see Tony walking along the side of the stream, head down and his hands thrust into the pockets of his trousers. He was whistling and his bulging satchel swung from his shoulder.

Tony, at fourteen, now attended the grammar school

in Ludthorpe. Anna still remembered the look of pride on Eddie's face when he had given her the news. 'He's passed the scholarship for the grammar. Bertha dun't know where to put 'ersen, she's that pleased.'

Anna had smiled. 'And so are you, Eddie. I can see it on your face.'

'Well, course I am. Can't deny it.'

'Is Tony pleased?' Anna had asked softly.

Eddie had shrugged. 'I reckon he is, but he ses all he wants to do is follow me onto the farm. But I tell him he'll have the chance to go to agricultural college now when he leaves there. That'd be something, wouldn't it?'

Anna had nodded, happy to see Eddie so pleased and proud.

Now, as she watched Tony come towards her, Anna realized how much he'd grown and matured in the last four years. He was a young man, already taller than her and almost as tall as his father. He had Eddie's brown hair and dark eyes.

As she saw that he was alone, she rose from her hiding place and waited for him to reach her.

'Hello,' she called and he looked up and grinned at her, his eyes wrinkling in just the same way that Eddie's did.

'Thought I'd come and see Maisie on her birthday.' He dug in his pocket and pulled out a small white paper bag. 'I've brought her some sherbet lemons. It isn't much . . .' he began, 'but she likes them and I've got her a card,' he added as if in apology that his gifts weren't more.

'That's lovely,' Anna reassured him.

Tony grinned. 'Went without me dinner today so I could get her a card.'

'You shouldn't have done that. What would your mother say?'

Tony tapped the side of his nose. 'She'll not know if you don't tell her.' He laughed. 'And you're not likely to do that, are you?'

Anna laughed too. 'Certainly not. Come on,' she said, picking up the buckets. 'Let's go and find Maisie.'

'Here, let me take those,' Tony offered, but Anna shook her head. 'No, I'm fine. That satchel looks heavy enough and, besides, carrying two I'm balanced.'

As they walked back towards the cottage, Anna said, 'She's been a very lucky little girl. Pat brought her a lovely doll and Eddie has made her a wooden cradle for it. They must have had their heads together planning it.'

Tony nodded. 'I know. He's been making it in the shed for weeks. It's from both of us really, but I wanted to get her a bit of something on me own.'

Anna laughed. 'They're her favourite sweets. The only trouble is I'll have to hide them from her and dole them out one by one.'

'Why?'

'If she eats too many at once – and given half a chance she will – the lemon makes her mouth sore.'

Tony laughed too and nodded ruefully. 'Yeah, I've done that too.' As they reached the cottage, Tony added, 'Is she inside?'

'I left her out here, playing with Buster. Oh, there he is. Look, halfway up the hill.' Suddenly, there was fear in Anna's eyes. 'But where's Maisie?'

Nineteen

Maisie skipped down the track towards the farm below her. There was no one about, so she climbed onto the five-barred gate leading into the yard and swung on it as she looked around her. It was lambing time; it always was near her birthday. Only yesterday a ewe had given birth in the field near the cottage. Her mother had allowed her to watch and the child had been fascinated to see a lamb sliding from its mother's tummy and within minutes stand on its own wobbly legs.

'Can we take it into the house to feed, Mam?' she had asked.

Anna had smiled. 'No, darling. This mother can feed her lamb herself. It's only when the mother can't feed her young for one reason or another that we have to do that.'

The child was disappointed, yet glad that the lamb would have its own mother. She wouldn't like to be without hers.

Now, swinging on the gate, she looked across to the large barn in front of her. She could hear the sound of sheep coming from inside. She knew that Mr Eddie, as she called him, took as many of the sheep as he could down to the farm when they were lambing. But he had too many to house them all. He never tired of telling her that she had been born in the cottage alongside several lambs.

Her glance swivelled to the back door of the farm-house. She ran her tongue round her lips, jumped from the gate and pushed it open. She skipped through it and across the yard. She hesitated only a moment before she raised her small fist and banged on the back door. A few moments elapsed before she heard a shuffling on the other side and then the door swung open and she was looking up into the unsmiling face of the large woman standing there.

Unfazed, Maisie looked her up and down then she smiled her most winning smile. Her dark brown eyes lit up and a dimple appeared in each cheek.

'Hello. I'm Maisie. I live over the hill in the cottage. Who are you?'

The woman gasped and blinked her small eyes rapidly. 'Well, I never did!' was all she could say.

'What did you never did?' the child asked innocently and completely unabashed.

'It's you.'

The child nodded. 'Yes, it's me. But who are you?'

'Who am I?' the woman repeated, rather stupidly it seemed even to the four-year-old girl. 'I'm Mrs Apple-yard.'

'That's Mr Eddie's name. Are you his wife?'

Her mouth dropping open, Bertha merely nodded, dumbfounded.

'What's your first name?'

'Bertha,' the woman murmured, as if in a trance.

Maisie beamed. 'I'll call you Mrs Bertha then. I like that. It's a nice name. Mrs Bertha.' She nodded as if satisfied by the sound of it. 'Can I come in?'

Wordlessly, Bertha stood back and opened the door wider, her gaze following the child as if she were utterly mesmerized by her small visitor.

'Ooh, it does smell nice in here. Have you been baking?' The child sniffed the air appreciatively as she stepped into Bertha's farmhouse kitchen.

'Er – well – yes,' Bertha said, waddling after Maisie. Already the child had hitched herself onto a tall stool near the table and was looking longingly at the scones laid out on a wire cooling tray.

To her astonishment, Bertha found herself saying, 'Would you like one?'

'Ooh, yes please. And please may I have some raspberry jam on it? I like raspberry jam best.'

Bertha cut open a scone, spread it thickly with butter and jam on each half. 'Wait a moment,' she said, bustling to the pantry. 'I've some cream here . . .'

A minute later she stood watching as Maisie bit into the warm scone, leaving a smear of jam and cream on her upper lip. 'Mmm, it's lovely, Mrs Bertha. Thank you.'

'You're welcome,' Bertha murmured. She sat down, her gaze fixed on the child. So this was that girl's child. The girl that Eddie had brought home four years ago and taken up the hill to live in his cottage near the wood. She stared hard at Maisie, trying to see any likeness to her husband in the child's face. She had brown eyes like his, but there any resemblance ended. Her hair was copper-coloured, almost ginger, and her features were nothing like Eddie's.

Of course, she probably took after her mother. Bertha screwed up her eyes, visualizing the girl. She'd had black hair and unusual eyes – a deep blue, violet almost, Bertha remembered.

That meant nothing. This child could still be Eddie's.

Maisie had finished her scone and was licking her finger and picking up all the crumbs on the plate. She smiled widely at Bertha, the line of jam and cream still on her lip. 'Are you Tony's mam?'

Bertha nodded.

'He's nice, isn't he? But he doesn't come to play with me very often. I 'spect he's too busy. My mam says he is. Doing his homework and helping his dad and you on the farm.' She paused and leant across the table. 'I'm going to school next year. I'll be five then.'

'So you will,' Bertha murmured absently, her gaze never leaving the child's face, her thoughts in a turmoil.

Maisie jumped down from the high stool and came around the table to stand near Bertha. 'I'd better go home. I'm not supposed to come over the hill. I 'spect Mam'll be ever so cross.'

She smiled as if the thought didn't worry her too much.

Then she put her arms around Bertha as far as she could reach and puckered up her mouth. Bewildered, Bertha found herself lowering her face towards the child to receive a jammy kiss. She was still sitting at the kitchen table, gazing after her as Maisie skipped out of the back door and across the yard.

'Well,' Bertha murmured, 'I never did.'

'Where can she be?'

Anna was almost wild with panic and Tony couldn't calm her down. 'Don't worry. She'll have wandered into the woods. We built a den in there last summer. I bet she's—'

'She's not allowed to go into the woods on her own,' Anna snapped. 'There's poachers' snares in there. Anything might happen. She knows that.'

Tony glanced up the slope again, frowning. 'What's the matter with Buster? He's never moved. I'd've thought he'd have come to us.'

'Buster,' Anna called. 'Here, boy.'

The dog rose reluctantly and came towards them, head down, tail between his legs.

'There's something wrong,' Anna said, her anxiety spiralling. 'Something's happened. I know it.'

Tony fondled the dog's head. 'What is it, boy? Eh?' he murmured. 'You'd tell us if you could, wouldn't you?' He knelt in front of the animal and held the dog's head between his hands. 'Where is she, Buster? Where's Maisie?'

The dog barked, pulled himself free of Tony's hold and began to run up the hill. A little way off, he stopped and looked back, then ran on again. Tony and Anna glanced at each other.

'I bet she's gone up there,' Tony said. 'He's trying to make us follow him.'

Anna's hand fluttered to her mouth. 'Oh no! She would never go up there. I've forbidden her. Someone – someone must have got her.'

Tony frowned. 'Got her? What do you mean?'

Anna did not answer. She was already running up the hill. Tony followed, his long legs loping easily after her. They arrived at the top together. At once they saw Maisie skipping merrily up the track towards them as if she hadn't a care in the world.

Anna ran towards her daughter, almost tumbling in her haste to reach her. 'Where on earth have you been?' She grasped Maisie's arm roughly.

'Mam – you're hurting.'

'I'll hurt you, you naughty girl.' Anna bent and

171

slapped Maisie's bare legs so hard that red imprints of her hand marked the child's calves. Maisie opened her mouth wide and yelled.

Watching, Tony winced as if he, too, felt the little girl's pain. Anna was still incensed, shaking the girl and shouting, 'Where have you been? Tell me where you've been.' But Maisie only wailed louder.

Tony moved forward and tried to prise her from her mother's grasp but Anna held on tightly. 'No, leave this to me. Come on . . .' She began to drag the screaming child up the track and over the hill. Maisie, tears running down her cheeks, looked back at Tony, whose tender heart twisted at the sight of her pitiful face. When they disappeared he turned and walked slowly down the hill towards the farm.

He must find his dad.

In the cottage, Anna stood Maisie on a chair in the kitchen, their faces on a level. 'Now, you will tell me where you've been or I'll smack you again.'

The child's wails had subsided to a hiccuping sob. 'To see Mrs Bertha.'

'Bertha?' For a moment Anna thought Maisie must be lying, but then she noticed the smear of jam on the child's mouth. 'You've been to the farm?' she asked incredulously. 'You've been inside the house?'

Maisie nodded. 'To see Mrs Bertha. She's Tony's mam. She gave me a lovely scone with jam and cream.'

The surprise was deflating Anna's anger. Whilst the child had deliberately disobeyed her, Anna knew Maisie could not be expected to understand *why* she should not go to the farm.

'Was she – was she nice to you?'

In a strangely adult manner, Maisie wrinkled her brow thoughtfully and then nodded. 'She didn't say a lot. I think she was surprised to see me.'

'I bet she was,' Anna murmured, lost for words herself. Then she pulled herself out of her stunned reverie to say, 'I'm not going to smack you again, but you've got to promise me that you will never go there again. If you do,' she warned, 'I will punish you very severely. Do you understand me, Maisie?'

The child had stopped crying, but her tears streaked her grubby face. 'Why can't I go and see Mrs Bertha again? *She* didn't say I couldn't.'

Anna sighed, unable to find a plausible explanation to make the young child understand. So she resorted to the age-old decree of all parents at one time or another. 'Because I say so.'

It was later that evening when Maisie was in bed in one of the upstairs rooms that Eddie knocked on the side door of the cottage. He stepped into the kitchen and without even greeting her, he demanded, 'What's been going on?' He was frowning and his tone held a note of censure. 'Tony told me you'd smacked Maisie.'

'Huh! I'd've thought you'd've heard all about it from Bertha.'

Eddie shook his head. 'Bertha's said nothing.'

'Maisie went to the farm. If she'll do that, she might take it into her head to go anywhere. She'll be going to the village before I know it.'

'She'll have to soon enough when she goes to school.'

'Oh no!' Anna shook her head. 'We're leaving before she has to go to school. In fact, I've made up my mind. I'll help you with the lambing and then we're going.'

'And where do you intend to go, might I ask?'

'Anywhere as long as it's far enough away from – from here, so that no one knows us.' Her voice dropped as she muttered, 'There's a few too many folks around here know us already.'

'Meaning?'

Anna ticked them off on her fingers. 'You, Tony, Bertha, Pat Jessop, Joe Wainwright and the other fellers who come at shearing and harvest. The doctor in town and the registrar, to say nothing of folks in shops when I've been forced to go into them. Specially the one in Wintersby. The gossip was rife in the village when I first came here. Mr Wainwright told me so.'

Eddie's tone softened. He could hear the panic in her voice. 'You can't live on a desert island, love. Wherever you go, you'll meet other people. And Maisie will have to go to school next year. I know you're bothered about her birth certificate, but they'll ask to see it wherever you go.'

'I'll say I've lost it.'

'They'll only get you to send to the authorities for another.'

Anna stared at him. She hadn't realized that copies could be obtained so easily. She sat down heavily on a chair and, resting her elbows on the table, covered her face with her hands.

'Why can't you stay here? I don't know who or what it is you're so afraid of. You've never told me.' There was a hint of reproach in Eddie's tone. 'But no one's ever bothered you, have they? Not in four years. Surely, you can stay?'

Slowly, Anna dropped her hands and stared into his face. Even though the thought of having to leave this haven and set off into the unknown frightened her, she shook her head sadly and whispered, 'I'm sorry, Eddie, but I daren't stay here. Not now. Not any longer. Not if Maisie's going to do what she did today.'

Twenty

Lambing was almost over. Only two more ewes left to give birth.

'You'll manage now, Eddie. You've been lucky this year. No motherless lambs for me to rear by hand in the cottage.' She smiled. 'Maisie's quite disappointed. She likes feeding them with a bottle.'

Eddie's eyes were anxious. 'You really mean you're going?'

'I'm sorry, Eddie,' Anna said huskily, 'but we must. I – I don't know how to thank you for all you've done for me. For us—'

'You could thank me by staying and making this your home,' he said gruffly. 'I'll even give you the cottage – and the bit of land round it – if it'll make any difference.'

'Oh, Eddie—'

'I mean it.'

She could see he did and tears filled her eyes. 'I couldn't possibly let you do such a thing. What would your wife say? And then there's Tony. It'll be his one day.'

Avoiding a direct answer about Bertha, Eddie said, 'Tony'd agree. I know he would. He doesn't want you to go any more'n I do.'

Anna touched his arm. 'You're such a kind man. I – I didn't know such kindness from strangers still existed

176

until I came here—' She broke off and turned away as if she was afraid of saying too much. 'We're going tomorrow,' she said with a finality that brooked no argument.

They were all packed, ready for the morning, their belongings in neat bundles and loaded onto Maisie's old pram.

'You'll be able to sit on the top if you get tired,' Anna told her, trying to make it sound like an adventure. But tears spilled down Maisie's cheeks. She cried silently, making no word of complaint, no screams of protest, but her anguish at leaving the only home she had ever known was evident on her small face.

'Come on, up to bed with you. We've got a long way to go tomorrow.'

'Where are we going?'

'You'll see,' Anna said brightly, making it sound as if their destination would be a lovely surprise, but in truth she had no idea herself where they were going.

They would just set off and see where they ended up, but after four years of comparative safety, even Anna was a little afraid.

It was completely different from the last time she had run away. Then she had not cared what became of her or of her unborn child.

Now, she did care. Eddie had taught her to care again.

In the middle of the night, Anna awoke to a dreadful noise. Buster was barking frantically and scratching at the front door to be let out. And from outside the cottage came the noise of barking dogs and the terrified bleating of sheep.

'Oh no—!' She flung back the bedclothes and dressed hurriedly. She climbed down the ladder and was pulling on her warmest coat when Maisie, bleary-eyed with sleep, appeared at the top.

'Mammy—'

'Go back to bed,' Anna began and then, with only a second's hesitation, she said, 'no, get dressed. As quickly as you can and come down.'

'Why? We're not going now, are we?' Maisie's lower lip trembled.

'No, but can you hear that awful noise? There are some dogs attacking the sheep. You must run to the farm for me and knock on the door as loudly as you can and fetch Mr Eddie. Can you do that?'

Maisie nodded eagerly, turned and ran back into her room to dress, whilst Anna lit a hurricane lamp and found her crook. She opened the side door and, as the child climbed down the ladder again, they stepped out into the darkness together, Buster streaking out ahead of them.

Outside the noise was even more frightening.

'Thank goodness,' Anna said. 'They're down there towards the stream. They won't see you. Now run, Maisie. Run as fast as you can.'

The little girl disappeared into the darkness and Anna braced herself to walk towards the terrifying noise.

In the moonlight, she could see two dogs attacking one of the ewes still in lamb. Already it was overthrown and unable to rise, helpless against the snapping jaws. Buster was barking and running at them, doing his best to drive the attackers away from the sheep. His sheep.

Anna moved closer and hit one of the dogs on the back, yelling at the same time.

The dog yelped in surprise. Intent upon their kill, neither dog had sensed her approach. The first ran a few yards and stopped, turning to stand and stare at her, panting hard. Now she lashed out at the other dog, but it jumped out of the way and turned to face her, head down and snarling.

They were big dogs, much bigger than poor Buster and in the darkness as terrifying as a couple of wolves. Crouching low, the second dog crept towards her. Buster stood beside her, growling a warning, but the aggressor took no notice of him. Anna held her crook horizontally in front of her to fend it off as it leapt up at her. She felt a sharp pain in her left hand and knew its white teeth, flashing in the moonlight, had bitten her. Now the other dog, emboldened by its companion, came closer. They lined up side by side in front of her, ready to spring. Beside her Buster whined and barked again.

'Down!' Anna cried in the firmest tone she could muster.

They took no notice and leapt in unison, but not at her. With one accord they fell on Buster, knocking him over. They attacked him cruelly, biting and tearing at his flesh. Now Buster was yelping in pain and fear. Anna hit out at the dogs with her stick and managed to frighten one away. But the bolder of the two turned and snarled at her. It grabbed her crook in its mouth, growling all the time. Gradually she drew it away from Buster, but then the other dog crept closer once more towards the injured sheepdog lying on the ground.

'No!' Anna shouted, feeling helpless to deal with both dogs at once. At that moment she heard a shout from behind her. 'Stand clear, Anna.'

She glanced back to see Eddie just behind her, pointing his shotgun at the dog nearest to her.

'Don't hit Buster. He's on the ground.'

'I won't. Drop your crook and move away.'

Anna did as she bade him. A shot rang out. Her attacker shuddered and fell to the ground. At the sound, the other dog ran, but Eddie levelled his gun and fired again. The dog stumbled, rolled over and lay still.

Now there was an ominous silence.

Eddie threw down his gun and held his arms wide to her. With a sob, Anna ran into them and was enfolded in his safe embrace. Behind them, watching, Tony stood holding Maisie's hand. As she became aware of them, Anna drew back.

'Are you hurt?' Eddie asked anxiously.

'Just my hand. It's nothing—'

'Let's take a look—'

'No, no—' Anna pulled away from him and stumbled towards Buster, lying motionless on the ground. Maisie ran forward.

'Oh, Mammy. What's happened to Buster?'

'The bad dogs hurt him, darling.'

Maisie squatted down beside the animal she considered her pet and touched his coat. 'It's all wet, Mammy.'

'Leave him, darling. We'll carry him home in a minute.' Anna rose and moved to where Eddie was bending over his sheep. 'I don't think we can save her,' he said, 'but she's gone into labour. Tony,' Eddie looked up and called across to his son, still standing motionless a few feet away, 'help Anna take Buster back to the cottage.' His glance rested on the little girl crying beside the inert animal. 'And take Maisie away from here.'

Silently, Tony did as he was asked. He spread out his coat on the ground and together he and Anna gently lifted Buster onto it.

'I ought to stay here and help your dad,' Anna said. She couldn't see Tony's expression in the darkness, but his voice was harsh. 'I'll come back and help him. He doesn't need you.'

Anna gasped and knew at once that Tony had read far more into the comforting hug his father had given her than had been meant.

'Tony, you don't understand—' she began.

'Don't I?' he muttered in a low voice so that his father should not hear. 'Oh don't I? Seems me mam was right all along.'

Anna shuddered and groaned. 'No,' she cried. 'It's not like that—'

'What's the matter?' Eddie's voice came out of the blackness.

'Nothing,' Tony called quickly before Anna could speak. 'I'll just help Anna and I'll come back.'

Without speaking to each other now, Anna and Tony carried Buster back to the cottage where they laid him on the hearth in front of the dying embers of the fire. Maisie knelt beside him. Now they could see that his black and white coat was matted with blood. The animal lay still, whimpering occasionally, his dark eyes wide and full of suffering.

'He's not going to die, is he, Mammy?' Maisie sobbed.

'Darling, I don't know.' Anna always tried to be honest with her child, even if the truth was painful.

Maisie sobbed louder. 'Can't we take him to the doctor?'

As if against his will, Tony's arm crept around the child's shoulders. 'We'll take him to the vet in the morning.' His glance at Anna was resentful, but he still kept his tone gentle towards the little girl. 'Dad'll take him.'

Suddenly Tony got up. 'I'll go back to him.' He left the cottage, slamming the door behind him. Anna winced but Maisie, unaware of the undercurrent of emotion between her mother and Tony, continued to stroke the dog's head. 'Don't die, Buster. Oh please don't die.'

A while later Anna heard the distant sound of a single shot. Shortly afterwards, the outer door to the kitchen opened and Eddie and Tony came in.

'The ewe's dead. I had to put her out of her misery. They'd nearly torn her throat out. There was no way even the vet could have saved her,' Eddie said as he came to where Buster was lying. 'How is he?'

Anna shook her head. 'He's still alive but covered in blood.'

'Right,' Eddie said, taking charge. 'Let's see to your hand first, love.'

He rummaged in the cupboard and produced bandages and a bottle of Dettol. As he bent over her hand bathing it and applying the bandage, Anna was acutely aware of Tony's morose expression as he watched his father's tender ministrations.

'You go home, Tony, lad. Thanks for your help, but—'

'No, Dad,' the young man said quickly. His glance rested upon Anna and his eyes narrowed. 'I'll wait for you.'

The following morning, Eddie arranged for the vet to visit Anna's cottage. He stood by whilst the man examined the dog. 'He'll live,' the vet pronounced. 'He's been badly mauled, but with tender care he'll be fine.'

He stood up and looked about him, noticing the bundles of belongings piled high on the pram at the side of the room. 'Going somewhere, were you?'

'We – we were leaving today.'

'Well, if you were planning on taking the dog there's no way he's walking any distance for quite a while.'

When the vet had left, Maisie looked up at her mother. 'Are we staying, Mammy?'

Anna sighed. 'It looks like it, Maisie,' she said flatly.

Despite the terrible events of the previous night, Eddie could not stop his smile stretching from ear to ear.

Twenty-One

'You've found another excuse to stay a bit longer then?'

Later that afternoon Tony stood in the centre of her kitchen, eyeing Anna belligerently.

She sighed, glancing down to where Maisie was sitting on the hearth beside Buster, lying in his basket. The little girl had not left the dog's side all day. Anna opened the front door and motioned to Tony to follow her. Once outside she said, 'Look, what you saw last night meant nothing. It's what anyone might have done in the circumstances. I'm sorry you saw it—'

'I bet you are.' The boy was disbelieving.

'It meant nothing,' she insisted. 'I'd have run to you if you'd held out your arms to me at that moment.'

'You're a bit old for me,' Tony said nastily and Anna closed her eyes, saddened to think that their friendship was at an end. Wiped out in an instant by an innocent hug of comfort between two friends.

'We're friends,' she tried again to explain. 'Your father's been very good to me.'

'Why?' Tony snapped. 'Just why did he bring you here in the first place? I can still remember how upset me mam was when he brought you home. I didn't understand it all at the time.' He paused and added pointedly. 'Now I do. She always thought there was summat more to it than he said. She even thought Maisie was mebbe his. Now – I think she was right.'

184

'I swear to you, on Maisie's life if you like,' Anna retorted angrily, 'that she is *not* Eddie's daughter.'

'Then whose is she? Tell me that.'

Anna's face blanched. She shook her head. 'No,' she whispered. 'I – can't tell you that.'

Tony's mouth twisted. 'You mean,' he said unkindly, 'you don't know.'

Before she had realized what she was doing, Anna's hand flew up and she smacked Tony's left cheek. 'How dare you say such a thing to me? If you only knew the truth—'

The boy had not even flinched or moved. 'Then tell me,' he persisted.

'No.' Anna stepped back as if even the thought of having to drag up the memories was abhorrent. 'It has nothing to do with you. Or –' she added with a last vestige of spirit – 'or with your father.'

Tony shrugged. 'Well, if you won't tell me, you can hardly expect me to believe you, can you?'

As he began to walk away, she cried after him, 'Why can't you just trust me?'

He paused and glanced back. 'Why can't *you* trust *me* enough to tell me the truth?' he countered. 'I know I'm only fourteen, but I'm not a child any longer. I'd understand, whatever it is. Unless,' he added pointedly, 'it's because you've something to hide. Something that you're really ashamed of.'

When she did not answer, he turned and walked away, leaving Anna staring after him. *If only you knew,* she thought, *how close to the truth you are.*

Of course, there was no way that Anna could leave now, even though after Tony's change towards them she would dearly have loved to go. But she could not leave Buster behind and it was impossible for him to travel in his weakened state.

Mid-morning she heard someone calling outside the cottage and opened the door to find Pat Jessop with her hand raised ready to knock.

The nurse beamed at her. 'Oh, you're still here. I was so afraid you might have set off early. I didn't want to miss saying goodbye, even though I do wish you weren't going.'

Anna sighed and gestured for Pat to step inside. 'We're not,' she said and quickly explained all the night's events that now kept them here.

'I really don't see why you have to go at all,' Pat said, lifting Maisie onto her lap and cuddling her. 'You're tired, my little love, aren't you?' Maisie leant against the comforting bosom of the district nurse, sucking her thumb. 'Why don't you go upstairs and have a little nap, eh?'

Maisie took out her thumb and looked up at Pat. In a serious, adult voice she said, 'I can't leave Buster. He needs me.'

'Of course he does, but your mammy's here and so am I just now. Nurses have to rest and look after themselves too, you know, else they can't care for their patients, can they?'

Maisie regarded Pat solemnly and then slid from her knee. 'All right, but you promise to look after him?'

'I promise and if I have to leave before you wake up, your mammy will stay with him until you do.'

They listened whilst the child climbed the ladder and then Pat leant across the table towards Anna. 'There's something you're not telling me that's upsetting you.'